Elizabeth Gail and the Secret of the Gold Charm

Hilda Stahl

 Tyndale House Publishers, Inc.
Wheaton, Illinois

Dedicated with love,
to
Tamara Langston

Library of Congress Cataloging-in-Publication Data

Stahl, Hilda, date
  Elizabeth Gail and the secret of the gold charm / Hilda Stahl.
     p.   cm.   — (The Elizabeth Gail series : 21)
  Summary: Twelve-year-old Libby is happy with her foster family and
wants to follow their Christian example, but she is reluctant to tell them
about the gold unicorn charm she has found.
  ISBN 0-8423-0817-2
  [1. Foster home care—Fiction. 2. Christian life—Fiction. 3. Family
life—Fiction. 4. Honesty—Fiction.] I. Title. II. Series: Stahl, Hilda.
Elizabeth Gail series : no. 21.
PZ7.S78244Eo   1992
[Fic]—dc20   91-25677

Printed in the United States of America

98 97 96 95 94 93
 8   7   6   5   4   3

Dear Reader:

Congratulations! You're about to go on a whole new adventure with Elizabeth Gail and her friends and family! Because this is an all new adventure, it is book #21. But the story actually takes place right after book #4, *Elizabeth Gail and the Dangerous Double*.

We hope you will enjoy reading about Elizabeth Gail and her great adventures. (A complete list of the exciting Elizabeth Gail books is shown on the next page.) And keep your eyes open for more *brand-new* Elizabeth Gail books coming soon!

The Elizabeth Gail series

1. *Elizabeth Gail and the Mystery at the Johnson Farm*
2. *Elizabeth Gail and the Secret Box*
3. *Elizabeth Gail and the Teddy Bear Mystery*
4. *Elizabeth Gail and the Dangerous Double*
5. *Elizabeth Gail and Trouble at Sandhill Ranch*
6. *Elizabeth Gail and the Strange Birthday Party*
7. *Elizabeth Gail and the Terrifying News*
8. *Elizabeth Gail and the Frightened Runaways*
9. *Elizabeth Gail and Trouble from the Past*
10. *Elizabeth Gail and the Silent Piano*
11. *Elizabeth Gail and Double Trouble*
12. *Elizabeth Gail and the Holiday Mystery*
13. *Elizabeth Gail and the Missing Love Letters*
14. *Elizabeth Gail and the Music Camp Romance*
15. *Elizabeth Gail and the Handsome Stranger*
16. *Elizabeth Gail and the Secret Love*
17. *Elizabeth Gail and the Summer for Weddings*
18. *Elizabeth Gail and the Time for Love*
19. *Elizabeth Gail and the Great Canoe Conspiracy*
20. *Elizabeth Gail and the Hidden Key Mystery*
21. *Elizabeth Gail and the Secret of the Gold Charm*

Contents

ONE
The gold charm

Libby blinked back tears as she slipped into the girls'
rest room. "I won't cry," she muttered through
clenched teeth. She'd forgotten all about her science
test, and Mr. Marston refused to excuse her. In five
minutes she had to be in class and take the test with
the rest of the sixth graders! If she failed the test
today, her nine-week grade would be a *D!* What
would Chuck and Vera Johnson say if she got a *D?*

Libby groaned. This morning at breakfast Chuck
had told Toby he wouldn't get his allowance until his
grade in reading improved. They would probably do
the same to her, or worse—stop her allowance al-
together. She had to have her allowance for camp
this summer.

Just then Libby looked up and caught a glimpse of
herself in the mirror over the row of sinks. Her hazel

eyes glistened with unshed tears, and her straight brown hair hung limply around her thin shoulders. She was tall and skinny and ugly! Mr. Marston probably wouldn't excuse her from the test because she was an ugly foster girl! The Johnsons loved her and wanted to adopt her, but nobody even considered that. It was even hard for her to believe. She'd been kicked from foster home to foster home after she'd been taken from Mother.

"I won't think about her," whispered Libby as she abruptly turned away from the mirror.

Suddenly she turned back. Something on the shelf above the sinks caught her eye. She looked closer. It was a gold charm from a necklace. She picked it up. "A unicorn," she said as she touched the pointed gold horn. The unicorn was about an inch long and was heavy in her hand.

The rest room door opened, and Libby heard two girls giggling as they started inside. With the unicorn clasped in her hand, Libby slipped quickly out of sight into a stall. She didn't want to face anyone right now. She recognized Gabby and Nedra talking and laughing, and she leaned weakly against the stall wall. They were the last girls she wanted to see right now! They laughed at her and made fun of her almost as much as Brenda Wilkens, her worst enemy, did.

"Do you think you left the unicorn in here, Nedra?" asked Gabby.

"I think so," said Nedra.

Libby froze. The unicorn belonged to Gabby Mercaldo!

"I sure hope so," said Gabby. "I knew it was lucky the minute I found it yesterday! It's a unicorn. Everybody knows they're lucky."

"I know," agreed Nedra. "I had it in English, and I got a perfect score!"

Libby frowned down at the unicorn. She'd never heard that. Was it true? If she kept the gold unicorn, would she pass the science test?

Gabby continued. "Last night I got home late, and my dad didn't ground me! And this morning my hair did just what I wanted it to."

Libby rolled her eyes. Gabby was always fussing with her long black hair.

"And when I had the unicorn, Chad Peters asked me to his party!" said Nedra, then squealed excitedly.

"The charm isn't here," said Nedra, looking under the long row of sinks.

"Maybe it's in your locker," said Gabby.

"Maybe. We'll look." Nedra paused. "Do you think you should turn it in at the office?" asked Nedra. "It looks expensive."

"It's only a fake gold charm like you can buy for a

few dollars! Besides, if I turn it in, the person it really belongs to might claim it. I found it; I'm going to keep it!" said Gabby sharply.

Nedra laughed. "So, keep it. See if I care!"

Libby gripped the unicorn firmly. The shiny gold horn bit into her palm, and she loosened her hold. Should she turn the unicorn in at the office? Her stomach knotted, and she shook her head. Maybe she'd turn it in after the science test.

A few minutes later Libby heard the girls leave. Slowly Libby stepped out of the stall. She knew she couldn't hide out in the rest room any longer. It was time for science class. She glanced toward the mirror as she started toward the door. She looked very guilty.

She looked down at the polished gold unicorn in her hand. A shiver trickled down her spine. Should she put the unicorn back where she'd found it? "No! It might help me pass my test," she whispered through a dry throat.

Was this stealing? She frowned. How could it be? It didn't belong to Gabby or Nedra. Besides, they'd said it was lucky, and today she needed all the luck she could get. She rubbed the unicorn between her fingers. "I wish I could pass my science test," she whispered. She pushed the gold unicorn deep into the pocket of her jeans and slowly walked out of the rest room into the noisy hall. Libby glanced around quickly to make sure no one noticed her or saw the guilty look on her face, but the others were hurrying to get to class before the tardy bell rang.

In the science room Libby sat at her desk near the window. A pleasant spring breeze blew in the open windows, taking away the usual stale air. Mr. Marston stood behind his desk taking roll. He was a short, stout man with blue eyes. When he bent forward to read the roll, his bald spot reflected light from the window.

Libby touched the pocket of her jeans and felt the lump the unicorn made. She glanced toward Susan then looked away. Susan wouldn't understand about the unicorn at all. Susan, Ben, and Kevin were the real Johnson children. Toby, another Johnson kid, was adopted. But Libby was still only a foster kid. The Johnsons were Christians, and Libby had become a Christian, too, a few months ago, but she was still learning how to live like Jesus wanted her to.

Libby frowned. Would Jesus want her to make a wish on a lucky unicorn? She pushed the thought aside as she glanced at Gabby and Nedra sitting in the front row up near Mr. Marston. They weren't talking or giggling. They both liked Mr. Marston and never did anything to make trouble for him. They didn't seem to mind that they didn't have the gold unicorn.

Finally Mr. Marston passed out the test. He walked back to his desk and sat down. "You may begin," he said in his deep voice.

Libby quickly read over the questions. Fill-in-the-blanks weren't as hard as she'd thought. The true-or-false questions seemed pretty easy too. It took her a little longer on the multiple-choice questions, but she finished just after the smart kids handed in their papers. Libby frowned. Could she really be finished already? That was very strange. She touched the unicorn. Maybe it was lucky!

With a satisfied look on her face Libby carried her test paper to Mr. Marston's desk. She smelled his after-shave and the strange odor of the marking pen he was using.

He cocked a gray brow. "Done so soon, Libby? You have ten more minutes if you need it."

Libby smiled smugly. "I don't need it."

Mr. Marston picked up her test and scanned it quickly. "No, I see you don't. I can't understand why you were so worried about it."

Libby shrugged and smiled.

"You have the first six correct."

"I thought so!" Libby walked back toward her desk. The unicorn really had brought her luck!

At a small scraping sound Libby glanced down at the floor. Timmy Oltz had stuck out his huge foot to trip her the way he'd done many times in the past. It was the first time she'd ever missed his foot! Usually she stumbled over it. Once she'd even fallen flat on her face and everyone laughed.

Libby stopped right beside Timmy's desk, looked down at him, and whispered, "Move it or lose it."

Timmy grinned and pulled his foot back.

Libby walked to her desk in a daze and sat down. She touched the unicorn in her pocket. This really was her lucky day!

TWO
The visiting museum

Libby glanced up as Mr. Marston stopped beside her desk. A shiver ran down her spine as he leaned down to her.

"You passed the test with a *B*, Libby," Mr. Marston said, smiling. "You should be pleased with yourself."

Libby rested her hand on the unicorn in her pocket and smiled. "I guess I was lucky."

He looked at her disapprovingly. "Lucky? I hope you're not counting on luck to get you through this class. You knew more than you thought."

As Mr. Marston walked back to his desk, Libby glanced at Susan. She couldn't wait to tell Susan about her grade, but she wouldn't breathe a word about the lucky unicorn.

Mr. Marston cleared his throat and asked for attention. "Class, immediately after you leave the class-

8

room you're to walk outdoors to a trailer, where there is an exhibit from the Museum of History. You may not run inside the trailer. You may not touch any of the items on display. You will listen to Mr. Gavin, the curator, as he tells about gold mining. When you leave the trailer, return immediately to your homeroom. Are there any questions?"

Libby looked around. She caught Susan's eye and smiled, then noticed Jamie Smith's hand raised high.

Mr. Marston rattled change in his pocket. "Yes, Jamie?"

"I visited a gold mine once," she said.

"That is not a question, Jamie."

The class laughed, but Libby frowned. She liked Jamie, and she didn't think it was nice to laugh at her.

Jamie grinned. "I want to know if they have stuff we can buy for keepsakes."

"They have tiny gold nuggets valued from two to five dollars," said Mr. Marston.

"Do they sell gold charms?" asked Gabby. "Like maybe gold bears or elephants . . . or . . . unicorns or something like that."

Libby stiffened.

"I didn't notice," said Mr. Marston. "We'll see in a few minutes. If there are no more questions, you're dismissed to walk quietly to the exhibit."

Libby slipped from her desk. Could the others see the lump in her pocket? She glanced down but saw that her jeans hung loosely on her and not even she could see the unicorn.

Just then Susan touched Libby's arm and whispered, "Libby, how did you do on the test?"

Libby turned to Susan with a wide smile. "I got a *B!* Mr. Marston graded it already because I was afraid I'd fail if I took it today."

Her blue eyes sparkling, Susan pushed her red-gold curls back from her oval face. "That's great! I know I passed it, too. I'm just glad we didn't have a math test today. I might not have passed it." Susan lowered her voice even more. "I don't want to see this dumb exhibit."

"I do." Libby fell into line behind the class with Susan right behind her. She'd wanted to see the exhibit on gold mining since the semi truck had pulled into the parking lot. Wide steps led up into the trailer. Usually Libby didn't like museum exhibits, but gold mining sounded interesting. The last exhibit to come to the school had been art, and she'd laughed at the modern paintings and sculptures.

Susan leaned forward and whispered, "Did you think of a way for me to get out of baby-sitting tonight?"

Libby frowned. She'd forgotten she'd agreed to

help Susan. "I didn't think of anything, but I will," Libby whispered.

"I just can't watch those two boys again! They're naughty and loud. The Grants let Al and Jake get by with everything! They don't even know how to obey."

"I could baby-sit for you," said Libby, thinking of her lucky unicorn as she slowly followed the line of students. "The kids will be good for me."

"They won't be," said Susan. "We'll have to think of something else—maybe a way for me to make the boys mind."

"Maybe." Libby followed the line outdoors into the warm spring day. A lone tree shaded part of the walk that led to the semitrailer that housed the exhibit. She glanced around Clay Barett in front of her and finally spotted Nedra and Gabby at the top of the steps at the door of the trailer.

"What are you looking at, Libby?" asked Susan.

"The kids in front," said Libby. She didn't want to mention Gabby, Nedra, or the unicorn.

Just then the janitor's helper, Bill Mason, stopped beside Libby. He brushed his dark hair back and looped his fingers over the black belt in his jeans. "Hi, Libby. Can you baby-sit my kids tomorrow after school?"

Libby smiled and nodded. "Mom said Susan and I

can baby-sit together since you'll be gone so late, if that's all right with you."

"Sure is," said Bill Mason. His blue eyes crinkled at the corners as he smiled at Susan. "Lori and Pete will have fun with the two of you."

"I wish all the kids we baby-sit were as nice as Lori and Pete," said Susan with a loud sigh.

"Having trouble with some other kids?" asked Bill.

Susan told Bill about Al and Jake Grant.

Libby and Susan knew Bill and his children from church. They'd been coming to church for five months, and Libby had had already baby-sat for them six times.

"I don't know what to tell you," said Bill. "I'll be praying, though." He glanced toward the trailer. "I'd better get going. Somebody spilled sand from one of the exhibits, and I have to clean it up."

Libby smiled and watched Bill hurry to the trailer. Libby turned to say something to Susan when Lissa Knotts, the girl standing behind Susan, wrinkled her small nose.

"I can't believe you're baby-sitting with that man's kids," said Lissa.

"Why not?" asked Libby, frowning.

"He's nice," said Susan.

"He was in prison, you know," said Lissa.

Libby gasped, and Susan cried, "No! I don't believe it!"

Lissa nodded and narrowed her brown eyes. "He just got out a month before he started working here. I don't think you should trust him."

"Why was he in prison?" asked Libby.

"For robbing a jewelry store," said Lissa.

"How do you know?" asked Susan.

"My dad knows. He's a policeman," said Lissa.

Libby's heart turned over. Should they baby-sit for Bill? She started to ask Susan but decided not to until they were alone.

"I don't know why they let Bill work near that exhibit," said Lissa. "There's valuable stuff to steal. My dad said some of the gold pieces are worth a fortune."

"The exhibit is guarded, isn't it?" asked Susan.

Lissa nodded. "But I bet Bill could slip something in his pocket without anyone noticing."

Libby bit her lower lip. "Did your dad say what kind of things could be taken?"

"The small things made from gold. Like gold watch chains, gold rings, charms—stuff like that," said Lissa.

Libby touched the unicorn in her pocket. Was it possible the unicorn had been stolen from the exhibit? But if it had, wouldn't everyone know about it?

A few minutes later Libby stepped inside the trailer. It was lit brightly and felt pleasantly cool inside. She heard a man telling details about mining, and she tried to listen as she looked at a chunk of rock with gold laced through it. She saw the pan used for panning gold and read the information about the miners. She listened as the curator told how miners used something called a cradle for sifting water and gravel to find gold nuggets. Slowly she walked down the aisle, looking at mining tools and items made from gold. She peered closer at several items in a display case then bit back a gasp when she spotted a unicorn the same size and shape as the one in her pocket. It was valued at $4,000. Had someone made a replica of the unicorn on display? And was it in her pocket right now?

"Keep going, Libby," whispered Susan, nudging Libby in the back.

Flushing, Libby walked to the last display case where several items were for sale to students. She looked for a unicorn, but there wasn't one for sale.

Finally she walked outdoors, her head spinning. Gabby had said the unicorn was fake. Libby breathed a sigh of relief. It would be terrible if the unicorn in her pocket was worth $4,000.

"That was so boring!" whispered Susan.

"I liked it," said Libby. "Did you see all that interesting stuff?"

Susan shrugged. "I liked the art exhibit better."

Libby rolled her eyes then moved closer to Susan as they walked toward the school. "Did you see the gold unicorn?"

"No. Where was it?"

Libby told her, but Susan only shrugged. To keep Susan from getting curious, Libby changed the subject. "Since you don't want to baby-sit Al and Jake tonight, why don't you call and tell them you won't do it."

"Because I said I'd do it," said Susan. "I can't back out at the last minute."

"I guess not. Maybe you could think of some games to play," said Libby. "Or you could take a video for them to watch."

Susan smiled and nodded. "Great idea! I'll do both! I just hope it works. Maybe Toby will let me take a couple of his games."

"He might," said Libby as she stopped at their homeroom door.

Just then Bill Mason walked past with a worried frown on his face. He opened the janitor's closet and looked inside then closed the door.

Libby watched Bill. She could see he was very

upset about something. He strode away before she could say anything to him.

Finally, Libby walked into her homeroom and sat at her desk. She pushed her hand into her pocket and thoughtfully fingered the gold unicorn.

THREE
The hiding place

Libby leaned back in the seat and stared out the bus window as the bus roared down the highway away from the school. Libby usually sat with Susan, but Susan had taken a different bus so she could baby-sit Al and Jake Grant. With Susan gone, Libby didn't have anyone to keep Brenda Wilkens from teasing and making fun of her. Ben was too nice to tell Brenda to close her big mouth.

Brenda's voice drifted up from the back of the bus as Libby fingered the gold unicorn. Brenda laughed and talked, but not once did she yell anything to Libby.

The bus stopped at the Johnson farm, and Libby jumped to the ground with Toby, Ben, and Kevin right behind her. The muscles in the back of her neck tightened as she waited for Brenda's usual remark. But Brenda didn't yell anything out the window.

With a sigh of relief Libby raced up the long drive after Ben while Kevin and Toby lagged behind. Goosy Poosy honked but didn't run at Libby. Ben stopped to pet the Johnsons' dog, Rex, so Libby was the first one in the house. She laughed softly. The unicorn had brought her luck again! Maybe the luck would continue, and they would have her favorite snack, apples and cheese. She called, "We're home, Mom! I'm going up to change."

"I have a snack ready in the kitchen," called Vera just as the boys ran inside.

Upstairs Libby closed her bedroom door, listened to make sure the boys weren't coming, then pulled out the unicorn. The curtains fluttered at the open window. The room smelled like fresh air.

Libby looked at the unicorn in the palm of her hand. The unicorn looked just like one she'd seen in a library book. It was very detailed. She touched the mane, the tail, the spiral twisted horn, and the loop on top that was made to hold it to a chain. Had it fallen off someone's necklace? Where had Gabby found it?

"It looks exactly like the unicorn in the exhibit," whispered Libby, suddenly shivering. But maybe if

18

they were side-by-side they wouldn't really look exactly alike.

"Gabby and Nedra were right. It is lucky," Libby said softly. "With the unicorn I'm sure to have good luck from now on." Maybe she could find a chain to hook it to so she could wear it all the time. But if the family saw it, they'd ask her where she got it. They might even make her return it to Gabby.

"Where shall I hide it?" Libby muttered as she locked her door and looked around her room. She spotted the puzzle box her real dad had sent her for her twelfth birthday. Before Dad had been killed in a car accident, he'd prepared the box for her with a letter to help her understand why he'd walked out on her and her mother.

Libby picked up the shiny puzzle box. The box opened by moving the pieces of wood in a certain pattern. Inside the box were hidden drawers. It would be a perfect place to hide the unicorn. No one in the house but Libby could open the box without the directions, and the directions were hidden in the toe of a shoe in her closet.

Quickly Libby slid the wooden pieces up and down, back and forth, in the right sequence. Finally the box opened. Carefully she tucked the unicorn in the small drawer then closed the box. She smiled in satisfaction. The box sat on her desk as if it didn't hold a secret inside.

Libby glanced at her Bible then looked away. It didn't seem right to have a lucky unicorn and the Bible on the same desk.

After changing into old jeans and a blue T-shirt, Libby ran to the kitchen for the snack Vera had ready for them. It was apples and cheese! Libby smiled then stopped abruptly at the tension in the air. She looked at the boys sitting at the table and Vera standing beside Toby's chair. Libby almost backed out of the kitchen, but she wanted to see what was wrong. Toby was probably in trouble again. Ben and Kevin were looking at him as if he'd done something really bad.

Libby sank to her chair. Toby had tears in his eyes, and he was clutching a thick pack of baseball cards to his chest.

"I found these in a brown paper bag on the playground," Toby said stubbornly.

"They're still not yours to keep," said Vera.

"They are mine!" cried Toby. "There wasn't a name on the bag!"

Vera shook her head and looked very stern. "Toby, tomorrow you will turn the cards in at the school office. You can't keep things you find. It's stealing just as much as if you'd taken something from someone's desk."

Libby's stomach tightened. Did that mean she'd stolen the unicorn? No! She'd taken the unicorn for luck. That was different.

Toby's lips quivered, and he blinked fast to keep back tears. "I can't turn them in! I want them too much!"

"Don't be such a baby," said Kevin, pushing his glasses up on his nose.

Toby sniffed, and Ben frowned at Kevin.

"He's not being a baby," said Vera. "He found something he wants. It's only natural to want to keep them. But we live by the rules Jesus made. We don't steal. Toby, you will return the cards to the office, even if it makes you feel bad."

Toby finally nodded. He set the pack of cards on the table and sighed hard. "When I get enough money, I'll buy every card I want!"

"That's fine," said Vera. She bent down and kissed Toby's red head. "You must do the right thing even if you don't feel good about it."

Libby reached for an apple. She would not return the unicorn no matter what! She bit into the apple. Juice sprayed. The apple was cold and crisp and tasted good. Life was perfect now. She had a gold charm to bring her good luck from now on.

"How was your day, Libby?" asked Vera as she sat down.

"I got a *B* on the science test," said Libby proudly.

Vera squeezed Libby's hand. "Good for you!"

"How did you like the gold mine exhibit today?" asked Ben.

"It was great!" Libby told Ben about the different things she remembered.

"Our class gets to see it tomorrow," said Ben. "I can't wait!"

"So do we," said Toby.

"We get to see it Thursday," said Kevin. "I want to see that gold unicorn that the kids were talking about on the bus."

Libby froze then relaxed when she realized Kevin was talking about the unicorn in the display, not the one she had. They talked about the exhibit for a little while longer, then Vera sent them out to do the chores.

Libby ran to the horse barn. When she'd first come to the Johnson farm, she didn't know how to do anything, but now she could do all the chores, even hook the milkers to the cows.

"Hi, Snowball," said Libby as she forked hay to her white filly. The family had given her Snowball for her twelfth birthday. It was the first horse she'd ever had. She had even helped train Snowball to lead and obey commands. In two years Snowball would be old enough to ride. "We'll have a lot of fun when I can ride you," said Libby as she hugged Snowball's neck.

Just after finishing the chores, Libby stepped out of the barn, flipped her hair back, and let the gentle breeze blow through it. A car drove into the driveway, and Susan got out. She ran right to Libby.

"How was it?" asked Libby.

"Much better! I checked a video out of the library, and the boys had fun watching it. Then we played ball in their backyard." Susan laughed. "Next time I'll take one of Toby's games and another video, too."

"I'm glad it went so well for you," said Libby as they walked toward the house.

"Libby!" called Kevin from the chicken house. "Can you help me a minute?"

"Be right there!" Libby turned to Susan. "I'll talk to you later."

Later Libby sat at the piano, carefully playing her lesson. She had to practice a half an hour a day. Sometimes she practiced longer. One day she'd be a concert pianist and play before thousands of cheering fans.

Suddenly Susan burst through the door and cried, "Wait until you see what I have!" Her cheeks were red and her eyes sparkling.

Libby laughed at Susan's excitement. "What is it?"

"This!" Susan thrust her hand out, and on her palm lay a shiny gold unicorn.

Her eyes snapping, Libby leaped up and grabbed the unicorn. "How dare you steal that from me!"

Susan gasped. "What do you mean?"

"That's my unicorn!"

Susan frowned. "Libby! What's wrong with you? I found this unicorn at school today in a box just outside the janitor's closet. I planned to turn it in at the office, but it was too late."

Libby stared at Susan in shock. "How can you say you found this in the janitor's closet? I know where you found it! How can you lie to me?"

Susan's eyes flashed fire. "I don't lie, and you know it!"

"I know you never did before, but you are this time!" Libby pushed Susan aside and ran from the room, down the hall to the wide stairs, and up to her room. She set the unicorn on her desk and grabbed her puzzle box. How dare Susan open her box and take out her unicorn?

FOUR
The surprise

Libby pushed against the wooden pieces of the puzzle box just as Susan burst through the door. "Get out of my room!" screamed Libby, looking over her shoulder at Susan.

"How dare you take that unicorn from me!" cried Susan, leaping forward.

"How dare you take the unicorn from my puzzle box!" Libby blocked Susan from grabbing the unicorn from her desk. "Don't touch that! I mean it, Susan Vera Johnson!"

"I'm telling on you, Elizabeth Gail Dobbs!" snapped Susan, trying to push Libby aside so she could reach the unicorn.

"I'm telling on you!" cried Libby as she frantically pushed and pulled on the wooden pieces. In her frustration she couldn't find the right combination to open the box. She wanted to bash the box against the floor. "You came in my room, and you opened my puzzle box!"

Susan stepped back and stared at Libby in surprise. "I did not! How come you think I did?"

Suddenly Libby thrust the box out to Susan. "Here! You open it! I can't."

Susan frowned as she took the box. "I can't do it without the directions."

"Then use the directions!" snapped Libby, trembling.

"But you hid the paper from me. I can't understand you at all." Susan held the box out to Libby. "Calm down and try to open it again."

Libby took a deep breath, forced her hands to stop shaking, and once again tried to open the puzzle box. This time it opened. She looked in the secret drawer then gasped in shock. "But how can that be?"

"What?" asked Susan, stepping close to Libby.

"My unicorn," whispered Libby through a dry throat. She lifted out the unicorn and laid it beside the one Susan had.

"Oh, my," said Susan weakly.

"They look exactly alike." Libby held them side by side in her palm. They had the same careful detail and were the same size. She held one in each palm

and weighed them. Hers seemed to weigh more, but it was hard to judge. "Which one is mine?"

"Does it matter?"

"Yes!" Libby frowned down at the unicorns. Hers was lucky, and maybe Susan's wasn't. "How will we tell them apart?"

"I don't know."

Libby opened her desk drawer and pulled out a thin red ribbon and laced it through the hook on the unicorn she thought was hers. "There," she said.

"Where did yours come from?" the girls asked at the same time then laughed.

Susan picked hers up. "I really didn't find this one in the janitor's closet. Timmy Oltz gave it to me. I almost didn't take it, but he begged me to. I said it was too expensive and nice, but he said he'd found it in the janitor's closet, and it was OK for me to have it." Susan shrugged. "So, I took it. But I think I might turn it in."

Libby didn't want to tell about hers, but she said, "I found mine on the shelf in the girls' rest room." She did not say that she would never turn it in or that it was a good luck charm. "They're probably cheap charms for a necklace."

"But they look very expensive," said Susan. "I'm going to show mine to Mom."

Libby's heart sank. "Please don't say anything

about mine. Please, Susan! I'll turn mine in someday, but not yet."

"You really should turn it in."

"But not yet! Oh, Susan, please! Not yet!" Libby's eyes filled with tears as she clasped her hands together.

Finally Susan nodded. "I won't say anything." Susan rubbed the unicorn's mane and sighed heavily. "I wish I could keep mine."

"Then do!"

Susan shook her head. "I know Mom will make me take it to the office. I know she will."

"Then don't show it to her," said Libby softly.

"Maybe I won't," whispered Susan.

Libby touched the unicorn. "It might be lucky."

Susan laughed. "Oh, Libby! That can't be!"

Libby shrugged. She knew it was.

"I think I will show it to Mom." Susan said. "I want to know if it's worth a lot of money." Susan cupped the unicorn in her hand. "I have a chain in my room. I'll hang it on that until tomorrow when I turn it in."

Libby quickly put her unicorn back in the puzzle box and ran with Susan to her room.

Susan pulled a gold chain from her jewelry box and hooked it through the loop on the unicorn's back. She held it out to Libby. "Here. Put it on me, will you?"

Libby draped the chain around Susan's neck, and the unicorn swayed across Susan's thin chest. Libby hooked the chain then looked at the unicorn. It looked beautiful against Susan's blue T-shirt. "It looks just like the unicorn in the exhibit we saw today," said Libby.

Susan gasped. "Are you kidding?"

"Oh, but it can't be that one! It was always locked away where nobody could even touch it."

Susan shook her head. "No, it wasn't! Didn't you hear? Someone in fifth grade asked to hold it, and Mr. Gavin took it out and let the kids pass it around." Susan's eyes grew round. "Do you think this is the one from the museum?"

"If it is, what about mine?" asked Libby hoarsely.

Susan shook her head. "I don't know! Let's go tell Mom! I wish Dad would get home right now!"

Libby caught Susan's arm. "Remember, you promised not to tell about my unicorn."

"I won't say a word, Libby. Now, let's go tell Mom!"

Libby hesitated then raced down the stairs after Susan.

They finally found Vera outdoors sitting on the picnic table with her feet on the bench and her chin in her hands. "Mom, look at this!" Susan said as she held the unicorn toward Vera while it still hung on the chain around her neck.

Vera gently held the unicorn. "Susan, it's beautiful! Where did you get it?"

Her stomach knotted, Libby looked at Susan, silently begging her to keep her promise. Across the yard Goosy Poosy honked and a rooster crowed.

"A boy gave it to me," said Susan.

"It's much too expensive to keep, Susan," said Vera. "It feels like real gold."

Susan gasped, and Libby sank to the bench, her legs too weak to hold her. Was Susan wearing a $4,000 unicorn stolen from the museum exhibit? Or could the unicorn in the puzzle box be worth $4,000?

Just then the boys ran up, and Susan showed them the unicorn. "Libby says it looks just like the one in the exhibit," said Susan.

Libby trembled. She knew how easily Susan told things she shouldn't tell when she was excited.

"How did you get it?" asked Kevin as he looked at it again. He wanted to be a detective when he grew up, so he always asked a lot of questions and tried to solve mysteries even if there weren't any to solve.

Susan quickly told her story again.

"It can't be the one from the exhibit," said Ben. "Timmy Oltz wouldn't steal it. And he'd never give it away if he did."

"Is it real gold?" asked Toby.

"Your dad will know," said Vera. "He knows real gold when he sees it."

"Will we be rich if it's real gold?" asked Toby.

Vera shook her head. "Susan must turn it in at the office," said Vera. "It isn't hers to keep even if Timmy says so."

"Oh, I wish it was!" cried Susan.

"Me, too," whispered Toby.

Libby locked her icy hands in her lap. Would they all go to jail if they had a stolen unicorn?

FIVE
A talk with Chuck

Libby sat quietly and looked around the dinner table. Two pieces of leftover fried chicken and a spoonful of string beans swimming in butter sat alone beside the empty mashed potato bowl and the empty tossed salad bowl. Wadded white paper napkins lay on the dirty plates. Libby looked at Chuck as he studied the unicorn in his hand. They were all waiting to hear what he had to say about the unicorn.

"It feels heavy enough to be solid gold," said Chuck with a slight frown.

"Solid gold!" cried Susan, her blue eyes round.

"Well, not exactly solid gold," said Chuck. "Gold is too soft to make into jewelry. You have to add silver or brass or copper or some other alloy."

"Let me hold it," said Kevin.

"Be very careful with it," said Chuck.

"Is it really real gold?" asked Ben as he looked at the unicorn in Kevin's plump hand.

Libby held her breath and waited for the answer.

"If I had nitric acid, I could test to see how close to twenty-four karat gold it is. As far as I can tell, it is a valuable piece of jewelry," said Chuck.

"Oh, my," said Vera weakly.

Libby's nerves tingled. If this was valuable, was hers? Or was hers an imitation?

Chuck stabbed his fingers through his red hair. "I don't know what to make of it. If it was stolen from the exhibit, how did it come to be in the janitor's closet?"

Libby shot a startled look at Susan. Susan had her hand over her mouth, and her eyes were wide. Libby turned back to Chuck. "Bill Mason is the janitor's helper."

"I know," said Chuck.

"What's the connection?" asked Vera.

"He's been in prison," said Libby hoarsely.

"In prison?" cried the boys.

"We knew that," said Chuck.

"Maybe he stole the unicorn!" said Libby sharply.

"I can't believe that!" cried Vera.

Chuck shook his head. "Neither do I. Bill is a Christian. He was a thief before he was born again, but no longer."

"Maybe the unicorn was too big of a temptation," said Ben.

Libby nodded. She knew all about temptation and giving in to it.

"Some kids at school think we shouldn't even baby-sit for his kids," said Susan as she pushed back her plate and rested her elbows on the table, her chin in her hands. "They say it's too dangerous."

"That's ridiculous," said Vera. "I can't understand that line of thinking at all! Bill paid for what he did. He's sorry for it, and now he's a Christian. Everyone should forget his past and accept him as he is now."

"That's not easy for some people," said Chuck. He looked solemnly around the table. "But it shouldn't be hard for this family. We want to live and love like Jesus. Jesus forgave Bill of his past. In fact, as far as Jesus is concerned, Bill's past no longer exists. We should act that way, too."

"That's right," said Vera, nodding. "So if kids at school say anything negative to you about Bill, tell them Bill is your friend and you trust him."

Libby laced her fingers together. Could she really forget about Bill's past and trust him? After all, Timmy Oltz had found the unicorn in Bill's closet.

"Timmy did find the unicorn in the janitor's closet," said Ben as if he'd read Libby's mind. "What about that, Dad?"

"We know Bill Mason. He is a man of integrity," said Chuck. "I'd look for another explanation on how it got there." Chuck leaned back in his chair. "I know we can't blindly trust him, we need to use wisdom." Chuck leaned forward and earnestly looked around the table. "We have Jesus to help us know when and who to trust. Remember that when you're in doubt."

Libby smiled in relief. It was good to know Jesus helped her even in that area. She wanted to trust Bill but not if he didn't deserve to be trusted.

"I'm glad it's all right to baby-sit for Bill Mason's kids," said Susan. "I like Lori and Pete. And I feel sorry for them because they don't have a mom."

Vera nodded. "Bill's wife, Abby, divorced him just after he was put in prison. She couldn't handle the humiliation. When he was released, she gave up custody of the kids so she could have a life." Vera took a deep breath. "That's hard to imagine, isn't it? I could never live without all of you!"

Libby was glad of that.

"Where's Abby now?" asked Susan.

"I don't know," said Vera.

"Bill said he heard she was in California," said Chuck. "She doesn't keep in touch with them."

Flushing, Libby whispered, "The kids are probably glad." She'd be glad if Mother never tried to talk to her. She wanted to forget Mother had locked her in a closet, starved her, and beat her. One time Mother said she was going to the grocery store, and she didn't return for days. Libby bit her lower lip. Maybe someday she could forget.

Later, after Chuck read the Bible to them and they prayed together, Libby walked to Chuck's study. She had to talk to him alone.

"May I come in?" Libby asked, poking her head in the open door.

Chuck looked up from behind his large oak desk and smiled. He'd changed into jeans and a blue and white striped pullover shirt. "Come right in, Elizabeth. I'll be glad to talk with you."

Libby perched on the edge of the desk.

"Anything in particular?" asked Chuck as he moved aside his paperwork. He owned the general store in town, and he always had a lot of paperwork.

Libby shrugged. She knew what she wanted to ask, but she couldn't ask him right out. "It's scary to think that unicorn was stolen from the exhibit."

Chuck nodded. "But we don't know for sure, do we? So, it's not worth worrying about."

"I know." Libby picked up a yellow pencil and studied it as if she'd never seen one before. "But it's still kind of scary."

"You'll know if it's the one when Susan returns it tomorrow," said Chuck.

Libby put the pencil in the holder and looked at Chuck. "If it doesn't belong to the museum and no one claims it, can Susan keep it?"

"I suppose," said Chuck. "But I'm sure someone will claim it. It's very valuable even if it isn't solid gold."

"I heard somewhere that a unicorn brings good luck," said Libby. She was proud of herself for sounding so calm. Not even Chuck would be able to tell his answer was important to her.

Chuck laughed. "I heard that, too. I heard a rabbit's foot is lucky, too."

"Is it?"

"Not a bit!"

Libby stiffened. "How do you know?"

"I know there's no such thing as luck!" Chuck walked around the desk and stood beside Libby. He slipped his arm around her shoulders and pressed his cheek on the top of her head. "It wasn't luck that brought you to us, Elizabeth."

"I know." She liked the feel of his arm around her, the smell of his after-shave, and even the slight smell of sweat. Down through the years she'd watched kids with their dads, and she'd always yearned to have a dad to love her, hug her, and talk to her. Chuck Johnson was better than any of her daydream dads.

"Prayer brought you to us," Chuck said firmly. He

kissed the top of Libby's head. "Some people might say luck brought us together." Chuck took Libby's hand and walked to the couch. They sat side-by-side like they'd done many times since she'd come to live with them. Sometimes he scolded her and other times just talked to her about herself. "There is no such thing as luck, Elizabeth. When something happens and you think it was good luck, it was probably a reaction to an action. You did something and caused something else to happen. Or it was God's law of probability. If you step out a window, you'll fall. God set the law of gravity into motion, and you can't go against that law without getting hurt."

Libby hugged a sofa pillow to her as she listened to Chuck. Was it possible the unicorn really hadn't made her pass her test or kept her from falling over Timmy's feet or kept Brenda from teasing her?

"Elizabeth, you know God is always watching over you. As Christians we are led by God's Spirit. It has nothing to do with luck. It has to do with listening to the still small voice of God inside us telling us what to do or what not to do. It's wrong to put your trust in something other than God."

"Why do some people believe in luck?" asked Libby, thinking of Gabby and Nedra.

"Because they don't know about being led by God, or they don't know about the laws God set in motion," said Chuck. Once again Chuck took Libby's hand. "It doesn't do a bit of good to make a wish on a rabbit's foot, a four-leaf clover, a unicorn, or even a piece of crystal. It's fruitless to wish on things. Things don't change situations or circumstances. Prayer does." Chuck looked at Libby closely. "Is there something you need me to pray with you about?"

Libby shook her head. She wanted to say, "Yes. Pray I'll have the courage to show you my unicorn. And pray I'll do the right thing." But she didn't say that. She didn't want him to pray about her unicorn. Then she'd have to give it up. When she was alone she'd decide what to do with the unicorn in her puzzle box.

"Don't worry about the unicorn," said Chuck.

Libby's stomach tightened. Could Chuck see right inside her head and know her thoughts?

Chuck gently tugged Libby's brown hair. "Susan will return it, and it'll all be settled tomorrow."

Libby bit back a sigh of relief. She jumped up. "I want to look at the unicorn again."

Chuck pushed himself up and laughed. "Just don't try to make a wish on it."

Libby flushed. "I won't," she said.

Later in her bedroom Libby lifted the unicorn from her puzzle box. "Are you lucky or not?" she

40

whispered. "Dad says you're not. But maybe he doesn't know."

Libby sank down on her round red hassock with the unicorn in her hand. Should she hide it away again, or should she turn it in at the school office?

SIX
The shocking news

Libby grabbed Susan's arm as the boys ran down the long driveway to wait for the school bus. The sky was overcast and the wind chilly. Libby shivered inside her warm jacket. "Susan, promise you won't say a word about my unicorn," Libby whispered.

Susan frowned as she tugged her jacket around her. "Libby! I already promised ten times!"

Libby sighed as she touched the unicorn in the pocket of her jeans. She heard the hiss of the bus brakes and trembled. "I know. Please, please promise again!"

"I promise!" Susan fingered the unicorn around her neck. "I will only tell about this one. Remember, you promised to go to the office with me to turn it in."

Libby breathed easier. "I will." No one would ever

know or even suspect she had.a unicorn just like Susan's.

"Hurry up, girls!" shouted Ben over his shoulder as he stepped to the open bus door.

Libby ran after Susan, and they sat side by side but didn't talk about the unicorns in case anyone heard them. Kids yelled back and forth. The bus smelled like tuna fish sandwiches and dirty socks.

At school Libby walked with Susan to the office while the other students were banging their lockers, laughing and talking. In the office Libby stood back as Susan walked right up to the high front desk where Miss Richie was talking on a white phone. She was the only worker in sight. The office smelled like someone had just sprayed lilac room deodorizer. Finally Miss Richie hung up and raised an eyebrow at Susan.

"I came to return something," said Susan. She didn't sound a bit nervous as she pushed back her long red-gold hair and unhooked the chain.

Libby moved from one foot to the other. Her stomach felt full of rocks. How could Susan be so calm?

"What is it?" asked Miss Richie, sounding too busy to bother with them.

Susan laid the unicorn on the desk. "This."

Miss Richie jumped and shrieked as if she'd seen a mouse.

Libby wanted to run out of the office, but she stepped up beside Susan in case she needed help.

"What's wrong?" asked Susan in alarm. She turned helplessly to Libby.

Libby shrugged. "Let's get out of here," she whispered.

Susan shook her head.

"Mr. Page!" cried Miss Richie, her eyes were wide and her mouth hung open. The principal's office was to the side of the front office, and his door was open.

Libby could see Mr. Page sitting at his desk, reading. He didn't look up.

"Mr. Page, come here right now!" called Miss Richie. "It's urgent."

Mr. Page dropped the paper he was reading and hurried out, straightening his pink tie. His brown hair was neatly combed, and his navy blue suit looked new. "What's wrong, Grace?"

Miss Richie pointed at the unicorn as if it would suddenly leap up and bite her. "Look! Susan Johnson brought it in."

Mr. Page peered down at the unicorn then shot a startled look at Susan, then Libby.

"What?" asked Susan weakly.

Libby pushed her icy hands into the pockets of her jacket. Something really terrible was happening. But what?

Mr. Page gingerly picked up the unicorn. "Come into my office, Susan. You too, Libby." Mr. Page cleared his throat. "Grace, call Mr. Gavin. He'll want to be here."

Miss Richie trembled as she picked up the phone and dialed.

"Into my office, girls," snapped Mr. Page. "What is your first class?"

"Math," they both said at once.

"Miss Richie, let the teacher know they'll be late," said Mr. Page.

Miss Richie nodded with the receiver pressed to her ear.

Libby forced back a shiver as she stepped into Mr. Page's office. The wide metal desk almost filled the small room. Two plastic chairs sat in front of the desk. Libby moved to the orange chair and Susan to the tan one.

His face pale, Mr. Page walked around his desk and dropped into his comfortable-looking, high-backed office chair. He carefully laid the unicorn on his desk in front of him. He cleared his throat. "This is very serious, Susan."

"What is?" asked Susan weakly.

Libby wanted to run from the room and hide forever. Before coming to live with the Johnsons, she'd spent a lot of time in the principal's office. It was never fun.

"This unicorn was stolen from the exhibit!" said Mr. Page.

The color drained from Libby's face.

Susan patted her heart. "Oh, my!" She sounded just like Vera when she was alarmed.

"Please tell me how it came to be in your possession," said Mr. Page.

Libby bit her lip. Because she was a foster kid he would've said to her, "Why did you steal it?" She was glad he didn't say that to Susan. It would've made her burst into tears.

Susan squirmed. "Someone gave it to me."

"Who?" snapped Mr. Page.

"Must I tell? I don't want to get anyone into trouble," said Susan weakly.

"Timmy Oltz found it and gave it to her," said Libby sharply. She didn't want Susan to get in any more trouble than she already was. Timmy Oltz could handle trouble. He visited the principal's office at least once a month.

"Libby!" cried Susan.

"It's better to be honest," said Mr. Page. He picked up his phone and told Miss Richie to call Timmy Oltz to his office immediately.

Susan frowned at Libby. "Why did you tell?" she whispered.

Before Libby could answer, Mr. Gavin rushed in. He gasped when he saw the unicorn. "You found it!" he cried as he scooped it up. "It's a good thing! I don't know what the museum would have done without this. It's one of a kind and can't be replaced."

Libby bit back a gasp as she gripped Susan's arm to keep her from blurting out about the unicorn in Libby's pocket. Why would Mr. Gavin say it was one of a kind when it wasn't? The unicorn in Libby's pocket seemed to burn her leg.

"I want to know who stole it, and I want him punished," said Mr. Gavin, with a stern look in his eye.

Just then Timmy walked in. He stopped short just inside the door and tugged his striped green and white pullover shirt over his jeans. "What did I do wrong this time?" he asked gruffly. He was almost as tall as Mr. Gavin.

"Where did you find the unicorn you gave Susan?" asked Mr. Page as he stood.

"This one," said Mr. Gavin, holding it in the palm of his hand toward Timmy.

Timmy flushed and wouldn't look at Susan or Libby. "I found it in the janitor's closet in a box on the floor," said Timmy.

"When?" asked Mr. Gavin.

"Just before school was out yesterday," said Timmy.

"Bill Mason stole it," snapped Mr. Gavin.

"You don't know if he took it," said Libby, frowning.

"He's an ex-con," said Mr. Gavin. "I might have known he'd steal it."

"No! He wouldn't steal it!" cried Susan, jumping up.

Libby moaned. Had he?

"Anyone could've put it in his closet," said Mr. Page.

Mr. Gavin started to speak then finally nodded.

"It could have been a simple mistake," said Mr. Page. "One of the students could have carried the unicorn off and, when he realized what he'd done, hidden it in the closet for someone to find and return."

"Is that what you did, young man?" asked Mr. Gavin, glaring at Timmy.

Timmy shook his head hard. "I found it in the closet! I did!"

"Why didn't you bring it to the office?" asked Mr. Page.

"I didn't think it was the unicorn from the exhibit," said Timmy. "I knew it looked like it, but I never thought anyone could get it out of the case."

Libby didn't know if Timmy was telling the truth, but she couldn't believe he'd steal the unicorn.

"I want to speak to Bill Mason," said Mr. Gavin.

"He had to help at the high school today," said Mr. Page. "You can reach him there."

"I'll do just that!" snapped Mr. Gavin. He strode out of the office toward the outer doors.

Mr. Page cleared his throat. "You children may go back to class now. Here's an excuse slip to give to your teacher."

Libby's mouth turned dry as she thought about Mr. Gavin talking to Bill Mason. If Bill had stolen the unicorn, what would become of his children?

Mr. Page thrust the note out to Timmy. "Get back to class. No loitering in the hall." He waved them out and closed the door.

Libby stopped in the empty hall just past the office and turned to Timmy. "Do you think Bill Mason stole the unicorn?"

"Libby! Don't even ask that!" whispered Susan.

Libby frowned at Susan and turned back to Timmy. "Well?"

"I don't know," said Timmy.

"Show us where you found it," said Libby, wishing Kevin were there to help her solve the mystery.

"We'd better get to class," said Susan.

"I'll show you first," said Timmy. "It won't take long."

Libby walked fast to keep up with Timmy. She

glanced over her shoulder and saw Susan finally follow.

At the janitor's closet Timmy opened the door and pointed to the floor just to the right of the door. "It was there in a little white box."

"Where's the box?" asked Libby.

"In my locker," said Timmy.

"I want to see it," said Libby.

"We have to get to class!" whispered Susan, looking fearfully around the empty hall.

"We have to hang up our jackets," said Libby as she slipped hers off while she practically ran to keep up with Timmy.

"You're right," said Susan, taking hers off as she walked.

Timmy's locker was only two lockers away from Libby's and Susan's. He turned the combination, opened the door, and pulled out a small white jeweler's box. He held it out to Libby.

She hung her jacket on the hook in her locker and took the box from Timmy. It was about two inches square and about an inch high. It could have come from any jeweler's shop. She turned it over and read, "Conway's Fine Jewelry. Little Rock, Arkansas."

"Bill Mason used to live in Arkansas," said Susan weakly.

Libby pushed the box into her jacket pocket and

closed her locker with a soft click. "Let's get to class," she said.

Libby flipped back her hair and lifted her pointed chin high. After school she and Susan would go to Bill's house to baby-sit his two kids. Maybe she'd find a clue to learn the truth about the unicorn.

SEVEN
Baby-sitting

With her jacket over her arm, Libby waited for Lori Mason to unlock the door. Lori was six, and she wore the house key on a chain around her neck.

"Daddy says it's always better to have a key in case he's not home when we get here," Lori said as she tried once again to unlock the door. A warm breeze ruffled her brown hair.

"Let me unlock it," said five-year-old Pete, handing his red jacket to Libby to hold. "I always can open it when you can't, Lori."

"Do you kids have to be home all alone sometimes?" asked Susan in surprise.

"Sometimes," said Lori as she held the key out to Pete. "We watch one cartoon and eat crackers, then Daddy comes."

Pete pushed the key in the lock and easily turned

it. He grinned proudly at the others. One bottom tooth was missing.

"Good job," said Susan.

Libby patted Pete on the back then followed the others inside. The smell of coffee hung in the air. The house had two small bedrooms, one bathroom, a kitchen, a living room, and a back porch big enough to hold the washer and drier and a small closet. The house was usually clean when Libby baby-sat, but no pictures hung on the walls, and the windows had only shades, no curtains.

Pete and Lori ran to change into play clothes while Libby walked to the kitchen to fix them a snack. Susan followed her.

"I have a great idea!" whispered Susan excitedly as she leaned against the counter near the sink.

"What?" asked Libby as she pulled a loaf of whole wheat bread from the refrigerator along with peanut butter and jelly.

"We can hang curtains at the windows and pictures on the walls and make the house look like a home. Wouldn't that be fun?" Susan's blue eyes flashed as she pointed to the window in back of the kitchen table.

Libby shrugged as she spread the bread out on the counter. "If Bill goes to jail for stealing the unicorn, they won't need pictures or curtains."

"Libby!" cried Susan in shock. "Don't even say that!"

Libby flushed as she smeared peanut butter onto the bread. She didn't want to think Bill was a thief. Somehow she had to learn the truth!

Just then Lori ran into the kitchen with Pete close behind her. They both wore faded jeans and blue T-shirts. "We're hungry," cried Lori. "We want ice cream!"

Libby laughed. "You always say that. And you always know you'll get a PB and J."

"That's a peanut butter and jelly sandwich," Pete said to Susan with a grin. "We didn't know that until Libby told us."

Lori jerked open the freezer and pulled out a half gallon of vanilla ice cream. "I'm having ice cream!"

Libby shook her head. "Lori, put it back."

Lori looked very stubborn. "No!"

Libby shot a look at Susan. Would Susan think she wasn't a good baby-sitter? When Libby saw that Susan was busy playing with Pete, she sighed in relief. Libby pulled the ice cream from Lori's hand and stuck it back in the freezer. She slipped an arm around Lori and smiled down at her. Libby had learned that Lori only got worse if she yelled at her or got angry. "Lori, I have your sandwich made."

Lori grinned. "OK."

A few minutes later they all sat at the table with sandwiches and milk. Libby listened to Lori and Pete as they told about their day. Pete went to a day-care center in the morning and then to kindergarten in the afternoon. He told about a little girl biting him because he wouldn't share a toy with her. Lori went the whole day to first grade, and she told about the reading group she was in and about being the best reader. At times Libby got bored listening to their stories, but she always listened anyway. Susan had told her it was part of being a good baby-sitter.

"Want to tell us about your day?" asked Lori, looking from Susan to Libby.

Pleased at the question, Libby smiled. It was the first time Lori had ever asked. She'd always wanted to talk about herself, and at times she'd stop Pete from talking so she could talk.

"I got an *A* in English," said Susan.

Libby couldn't think of anything but the unicorn, but she couldn't say anything about it. Finally she said, "I played volleyball in gym then had to take a shower." She hated taking showers after gym.

Later Susan read to the kids while Libby cleaned up the kitchen. She always washed the dishes left in the sink and swept the kitchen floor. Sometimes she washed a load or two of clothes or folded what was left in the drier. She checked the drier and pulled the clothes out and let them drop into the blue plastic basket. Quickly she folded them then carried them to the bedrooms. Now was her chance to look around! She put Lori's and Pete's clothes away first then took Bill's to his room. A tingle ran down her spine as she put the pile neatly on the foot of his bed then walked to his closet and opened it. Libby took a deep breath and steeled herself to look. She knew it was wrong to search Bill's room, but she had to make sure he wasn't still a thief.

Libby glanced around the almost empty closet, found nothing then checked the dresser. She found a folded newspaper clipping in a drawer with a belt and a tie pin. She picked up the clipping to read it. Her eyes almost popped out of her head. It was a paper from Little Rock, and the story was about the robbery at Conway's Fine Jewelry! It said Bill Mason was given a four-year sentence with a chance of parole at the end of eighteen months.

"Conway's Fine Jewelry," Libby whispered hoarsely. The box Timmy had found the unicorn in had been from Conway's! Had Bill taken the unicorn from the exhibit? And was the unicorn in her pocket also stolen?

Quickly Libby put the clipping in place and shut the drawer. She took a deep, steadying breath and walked to the living room. How she wanted to tell

Susan to follow her to the kitchen, but she didn't want the kids to hear her. She looked intently at Susan, her eyes full of the unspoken message.

Susan glanced up from the book then quickly finished it, and turned on a cartoon for the kids to watch. "I'm going to the kitchen with Libby," said Susan.

The kids were engrossed in the cartoon and didn't answer.

Almost bursting with her news, Libby led the way to the kitchen and sank into a kitchen chair.

"You look scared," whispered Susan. "What's wrong?"

Libby quickly told her what she had found in Bill's drawer. "I think he's guilty!"

"No! I think somebody is trying to frame him," said Susan in a low, tight voice. "He wouldn't really be dumb enough to use a box from Conway's. Think about it, Libby! Would he do that?"

"You could be right," said Libby with a thoughtful look. "It would be dumb to use the Conway's box. We'll keep it a secret until we know more. If we give it to Mr. Gavin, he'll try to have Bill arrested. It would hurt Pete and Lori a lot."

Susan nodded hard. "It would!"

Libby tapped her fingers on the arm of the chair. "What if he is guilty, Susan?"

58

"He's not!" Susan shivered. "He just can't be! I won't think about it!" Susan jumped up. "I'll go read the kids another story while you make supper."

Libby nodded. It was easy enough to open a can of chicken noodle soup for soup and crackers.

As she fixed the soup she remembered Chuck saying it was very important to pray for others in trouble. Silently she prayed for Bill and the kids. "And heavenly Father, show Susan and me how we can help them the most."

Later, after Pete and Lori were asleep for the night, Susan and Libby sat on the couch and talked about what they could do to prove Bill had not stolen the unicorn. They couldn't find an answer, so they talked about how they could fix the house to look more like a home.

"I'll call Mom and ask her about curtains," said Susan.

"And I'll see if there are some pictures around here we could hang. There are nails in the wall where pictures used to hang," said Libby as she pointed to a nail above the couch between two windows.

While Susan called Vera, Libby looked in the closet on the back porch. She found an empty frame and carried it to the kitchen table. What could she use as a picture? She glanced at the refrigerator. A paper covered with swirls Lori had fingerpainted was held in place by magnets. With a low laugh Libby took down the picture and fit it in the frame. She had to cut the picture down a little, but it still looked good, and she knew no one could tell she'd had to trim it off.

Libby hung it over the couch then stepped back to admire her work. It looked bright and beautiful. The wall was painted an off-white, so the blue, lavender, purple, red, and white swirls in the painting brightened the room.

Susan walked in, stopped short, and stared at the picture. With a laugh she ran to it. "Libby, it's great! Lori will be proud to see it there."

"I think Bill will like it too," said Libby.

"I do, too!" Susan clasped her hands, and her blue eyes sparkled. "Mom said she has curtains that will work in here. She said Dad has to come into town in a few minutes and will drop them off for us." Suddenly Susan sobered. "Libby, you should show Dad the box."

Libby thought about it for a minute then nodded. "I guess I should."

"And the unicorn," said Susan softly.

Libby pushed her hand into her pocket and touched the unicorn. She wasn't ready to give it up, and she knew Chuck would make her. "I'll tell him another day," she said stiffly.

Susan sighed. "All right. It sure is strange that Mr. Gavin says there's only one unicorn like his. I couldn't see any difference at all in the one you have and the one I returned."

"I wish we could have it checked." Libby sat on the couch with the unicorn in her hand. She'd forgotten to see if it brought her good luck today.

"I heard Gabby and Nedra talking today," said Susan as she sat beside Libby. "They think the unicorn I handed in was the one they had, but they wouldn't go tell Mr. Gavin about it because they might get in trouble."

"I'd sure like to know where Gabby found it," said Libby. "How could I ask her without making her suspicious?"

"I don't know, but you'll think of something."

Just then someone knocked on the door, and Libby jumped up. She pushed the unicorn into her pocket then ran to the door. It was Chuck with a bag full of curtains.

"Hi, girls," Chuck said. His red hair was wind blown, and he looked tired.

"Can you come in a while?" asked Susan as Chuck set the bag on the couch.

"Sure," he said, brushing his hair in place with his hand. "How's it going? Mom told me about the unicorn and your visit to the office."

"We have something to show you, Dad," said Susan, looking quickly at Libby. "Right, Libby?"

Libby nodded. She opened the closet and pulled the white box from her jacket pocket. She handed it to Chuck and told him where it had come from. "And we know that Bill's last robbery was at Conway's in Little Rock."

Chuck whistled in surprise as he studied the box. "It seems pretty stupid to put the unicorn in here and hide it in his closet at school. It sounds like somebody is framing him."

Libby and Susan looked at each other and laughed then said together, "That's what we said!"

"I'll take this and go talk to Dave Knotts. He's a policeman; he'll know what we should do."

"He won't tell Lissa, will he?" asked Susan. Dave Knotts was Lissa's dad.

"No," said Chuck. "He'll know what to do without making trouble for Bill. Dave wants to see Bill make it as much as we do."

Libby touched her unicorn and almost pulled it out to show it to Chuck then changed her mind. What did it matter that she kept her unicorn a secret a while longer? She had another test in science Friday, and she needed it then.

She walked restlessly around the room. The unicorn suddenly seemed to weigh a ton.

EIGHT
Bill's answers

Libby sat quietly beside Susan on the couch in Bill Mason's living room. Bill hadn't noticed the picture or the curtains, but Libby didn't care. She was more interested in hearing what Bill was saying to Chuck. Libby glanced to where Chuck was sitting in the faded overstuffed chair and Bill in the rocker. She didn't dare make a sound because Chuck might make them wait in the car for him. Chuck had come to pick them up but had asked Bill if he could talk with him first.

Susan pressed her hand over a yawn, but Libby knew she wouldn't let herself fall asleep. She wanted to hear Bill's answers too.

"Chuck, I'm glad you believe I'm innocent," said Bill.

Chuck held the jeweler's box out to Bill. "Susan said the unicorn was in this," said Chuck.

"You don't say!" Bill examined the box and shook his head. "I never had such a box. You probably know I robbed that jewelry store, but I didn't take any boxes."

Chuck nodded and took the box back. "I know the unicorn is valuable, but it doesn't seem valuable enough for a jewel thief to bother with."

"On its own it's not. It's part of a collection," Bill sighed heavily. "I heard about the collection while I was in prison, so I can't say I didn't know about it."

Libby forced herself to stay relaxed and not to lean eagerly forward. She didn't want to miss a word.

"Tell me about it," said Chuck.

"In 1880 Josef Mueller took some of the gold he'd mined and crafted four special charms, one for each of his daughters. He used copper with the gold to keep the shiny gold look. The unicorn was one of the charms he crafted. He also made a Pegasus, a mermaid, and a nymph. With the four of them together again in one collection, they'd be priceless. Some collectors would give anything to have all four."

Libby bit her lip to keep back a gasp.

"Is the unicorn in the museum exhibit from this collection?" asked Chuck.

"Yes." Bill brushed his fingers through his dark

hair. "I didn't know it was there until I saw the exhibit the day they set up. I couldn't believe they'd take it around to schools to show it. It's an invitation to thieves."

"I wondered about that myself," said Chuck.

Libby wanted to ask who had chosen what to bring in the exhibit, but she didn't risk it.

"Where are the other pieces to the collection?" asked Chuck.

Bill shook his head. "I don't know. I heard a collector has the others and would do anything for the unicorn, but I don't know it for a fact."

Chuck absently tapped the small white box with a finger. "Does Mr. Gavin know about the collection?"

"I'm sure he does," said Bill. Then he turned to Libby and Susan. "Did Mr. Gavin mention Josef Mueller and his gold charms?"

Susan shrugged. "I didn't listen to him."

Libby frowned thoughtfully. "If he did, I don't remember."

"Someone should find out," said Bill. "If I act curious, I'll be suspected even more."

Right then Libby decided to find the answer herself. Tomorrow she'd ask Mr. Gavin. She shivered just thinking about it.

"Bill, have you seen all of the charms?" asked Chuck.

"No," said Bill. "They were out of my league. You'd have to have a special buyer for them, and I never moved in those circles."

Libby hadn't thought about different circles of thieves. It seemed strange.

"Could there be two unicorns in the collection?" asked Susan.

Libby froze, but didn't look at Susan in case she gave herself away. The unicorn in her pocket suddenly seemed to fill the whole room.

Bill shook his head. "No, but there's always a possibility someone forged a unicorn."

Libby bit back a gasp. A forged unicorn!

"It would be a smart move," said Bill.

"Why?" asked Chuck.

"The thief could have a forgery made then switch unicorns in the exhibit, and no one would ever know the difference—unless someone was suspicious and tested them both with nitric acid."

"How would they do that?" Libby asked, trying to sound calm.

"It's pretty simple," Bill answered. "Gold is one of the few metals that doesn't react to nitric acid. If almost any other metal gets nitric acid on it, it will bubble and foam and change colors. But when you put a drop of nitric acid on gold, it doesn't do anything. So what people do is file a small part of what they want to test, and then put a small drop of nitric acid on it. If nothing happens, it's real gold."

Libby suddenly knew she had to find nitric acid and test the unicorn in her pocket.

Later, just as they were leaving, Bill exclaimed, "Curtains! And Lori's painting! I can't believe you girls went to so much trouble."

Libby swelled with pride, and she saw Susan did the same. "We wanted to," said Libby.

"We're glad you like what we did," said Susan.

Bill hugged them both and thanked them again. He turned to Chuck. "You should be very proud of your girls."

"I am," said Chuck.

Libby felt the happiness slip away. He wouldn't be proud of her if he knew about the unicorn in her pocket.

"Libby, will you baby-sit again tomorrow after school for a couple of hours?" asked Bill.

Libby nodded. She was afraid if she opened her mouth to speak, she'd pour out the story about her unicorn.

The next morning Libby picked up her Bible before she went to school and started to read, but her mind drifted. She thought of the unicorn and the test she wanted to do well on and the question she wanted to ask Mr. Gavin. She closed her Bible, started to pray, then stopped mid-sentence as her mind drifted to the problem of getting nitric acid.

"The science lab! They might have it!" Libby leaped up and ran from her room with the unicorn safely in the pocket of her jeans. She suddenly couldn't wait to get to school to see if she could find nitric acid and to learn what she could from Mr. Gavin.

Later, as she stepped up in the school bus, she spotted Gabby sitting with Brenda. There was an empty seat behind them. Libby touched the unicorn in her pocket. Once again it had brought her good luck!

With a smile Libby sat behind Gabby and Brenda. They were so deep in conversation they didn't notice her. Susan sat with Becky Little to talk about a special Sunday school project, so Libby had the seat to herself. "What luck!" she whispered. Why, with the unicorn everything would go right for her from now on! She'd never have to be afraid again!

Just then Libby remembered her talk with Chuck. He'd said there was no such thing as luck. Another time when she was afraid he'd told her fear came from Satan. He'd helped her memorize 2 Timothy 1:7, "For God hath not given us the spirit of fear; but of power, and of love, and of a sound mind."

Libby squirmed uneasily. Could she trust God as

well as the gold unicorn? She frowned. It wasn't a question she needed to answer, so why bother thinking about it?

In the seat in front of Libby, Gabby said to Brenda, "I'll tell you something about the unicorn if you don't tell."

"What?" asked Brenda excitedly.

Libby held her breath. She didn't want to make a single sound that would make Gabby or Brenda turn around and notice her.

"I found the unicorn and kept it for a whole day!"

Libby locked her icy hands in her lap.

"Where did you find it?" asked Brenda.

"In the janitor's closet. I went to get a rag for Miss Weaver, and I saw it, so I took it." Gabby told about the unicorn bringing her good luck then loaning it to Nedra for good luck. "But then Nedra lost it, and I guess Susan Johnson found it and turned it in."

"You actually held the unicorn in your hand?" Brenda giggled then sighed. "I wish you would've showed it to me."

"I planned to, but Nedra lost it."

Libby listened until they started talking about boys, then she thought of a plan to go to the science lab and test the unicorn. Lunchtime would be the only chance she'd have. She'd do it then! She shivered at the daring thought.

At lunchtime Libby slipped away from the line in the cafeteria and ran lightly down the empty hall toward the science room. She was glad her sneakers didn't make any noise on the polished floor. Silently she opened the door and slipped into the science room. She could smell some kind of acid, and she wrinkled her nose. Sunlight streamed in the windows.

Her heart in her mouth, she walked to the cabinet to look for nitric acid. Trembling, she quickly looked at the labels and couldn't find nitric acid. Her shoulders slumped in disappointment. "I'll look again," she muttered. She knew how easy it was to overlook things, especially when she was nervous.

She took a deep breath, then coughed from the smells, and looked again.

Suddenly the science room door opened, and Libby's legs almost gave way. Mr. Marston walked in, and Libby wanted to sink through the floor.

"What are you doing?" asked Mr. Marston sharply.

"Looking for something," said Libby with a crack in her voice.

"I can see that," said Mr. Marston. "Exactly what are you looking for?"

Before she could stop herself, Libby blurted out, "Nitric acid."

"We don't have any. Why do you want it?"

"An experiment," said Libby weakly.

"I'm glad to see you're trying to bring your grade up with extra credit, but you'll have to try something else." Mr. Marston pushed the door open wider. "I have papers to grade, so run along."

Libby walked out, her legs shaky and her stomach a hard knot. Why had she said anything about nitric acid? What if Mr. Marston got suspicious? Libby groaned.

Just then Libby saw Mr. Gavin at the pay phone outside the cafeteria. His back was to her. The unicorn in her pocket seemed like a bright beacon of light, drawing attention to her pocket. "I can't let him see me," she whispered, frantically looking around for a place to hide. She saw the janitor's closet door open slightly and decided to slip inside until Mr. Gavin finished talking on the phone.

Libby ran toward the closet then hesitated, her heart racing. Could she hide inside without thinking about the terrible times Mother had locked her in? Libby frowned. She either had to run back down the hall or hide inside the closet. She couldn't hesitate a second longer in case Mr. Gavin turned around and saw her. Shivering slightly, she eased through the opening into the closet. She could stand it as long as the door was open.

Suddenly she realized she could hear Mr. Gavin

talking. She tried not to listen, but when he mentioned the unicorn, she strained to hear every word.

"It's a copy, but I'm keeping it to myself for a while. I have a plan in motion," he said.

Libby swayed weakly and almost knocked over a pail, making her miss his plan.

The unicorn he had was a copy! Libby touched the unicorn in her pocket. Her unicorn was the real one! If anyone learned she had it, she might be sent to prison for life!

NINE
Baby-sitting again

The sun hot on her head, Libby ran after Lori and
Pete as they raced to the swings in the park. Boys and
girls played soccer in the center of the park while
teens played tennis on the tennis court. A truck
drove past, covering the sounds of shouts and laugh-
ter for a brief moment.

Lori and Pete reached the swings at the same time
then both yelled, "Push me, Libby!"

Libby pushed them in turn while her brain whirled
with what to do about the unicorn in her pocket. She
knew she could never keep it even if it brought good
luck, but she didn't know how to return it without getting in trouble. She'd not found the courage to ask Mr.
Gavin about Josef Mueller's four charms. Maybe
tomorrow. Tomorrow was Friday, and she had to do

something before school was out. The exhibit was pulling out Friday after school to go to another town.

Just then Libby heard girls laughing and talking off to her right. She glanced at them then groaned. It was Gabby and Nedra, and they were heading right toward her! Had her lucky unicorn turned on her?

Libby quickly stopped Pete's swing. "Kids, let's run to the slide," she said.

Pete jumped out immediately and ran to the slide, but Lori stayed stubbornly in the swing.

"I want to swing!" Lori snapped.

"Then swing!" said Libby. "I'll go with Pete."

"I want you to swing me!" shouted Lori as loud as she could.

Libby flushed as she hesitated between the swings and the slide.

"Having trouble, Libby?" asked Gabby with a wicked laugh.

"Don't you know how to baby-sit?" asked Nedra with a flip of her hair.

Libby didn't answer but angrily pushed Lori high. Libby wanted to tell Gabby and Nedra to leave her alone.

"I can't believe you'd baby-sit that terrible man's kids," said Nedra, pushing back her blonde hair.

"Are you talking about my dad?" asked Lori sharply.

Libby frowned at Nedra. "Don't say another word about him!"

"What about my dad?" cried Lori, trying to stop the swing. "Stop me, Libby! Stop me right now!"

Libby caught the chains and jerked Lori to a stop. "Go play with Pete," she said, pushing Lori away from Nedra and Gabby.

"I bet your dad stole that unicorn," said Gabby.

"Stop it!" cried Libby.

"What unicorn?" asked Lori, her face red and tears filling her brown eyes.

"And he should go to prison!" said Nedra.

"No!" Lori ran at Nedra and pushed hard against her.

Nedra stumbled but grabbed the leg of the swing and caught herself. "Don't be such a brat!" snapped Nedra. "You know your dad is a thief! So don't act like he's not."

Gabby turned to Libby. "Why do you baby-sit for Bill Mason?"

"He's not a thief!" cried Libby angrily. "But maybe you are! You had the unicorn!" Libby wanted to grab the words back the minute she said them.

Gabby's face turned as white as the clouds in the bright spring sky. "That's a lie!"

"Who told you she had it?" asked Nedra in alarm.

"Nedra!" cried Gabby.

"You had the unicorn," said Libby.

"Bill Mason stole it!" snapped Gabby.

Lori burst into wild tears and grabbed Libby's hand. "I don't like those girls! Take me home!"

Just then Pete ran up. "Why are you crying, Lori? Did Libby hurt you?"

"No!" snapped Libby.

"That girl says Dad's going to prison again," said Lori between sobs as she pointed at Gabby.

"That's a lie!" yelled Pete, doubling his fists at his sides. "He promised he wouldn't ever go again!"

"You can't believe anything he says," said Gabby with a toss of her long black hair.

Libby glared at Gabby. "Stop it! You're scaring the kids."

Gabby shrugged. "I'm just telling the truth."

"We always tell the truth," said Nedra.

"You didn't tell Mr. Gavin you had the unicorn," snapped Libby. "I just might tell him tomorrow!"

Gabby took a menacing step toward Libby. "If you tell him that, I'll tell him you're lying to cover up for Bill Mason."

"He'll believe us," said Nedra. "Nobody would believe a foster kid!" Nedra caught Gabby's arm and tugged. "Let's get out of here. We don't want anybody to think we're friends with her!"

"And you better not tell anyone about my having

that unicorn, Libby," snapped Gabby. "If you do, I'll tell them you helped Bill Mason steal it! Who do you think they'll believe?"

Libby wanted to punch Gabby, but she didn't.

"Nobody would believe a kid without a real family," said Nedra with a sneer.

Libby flushed but didn't have time to feel sorry for herself because Lori and Pete clung to her and begged her to take them home. She knew it was her job to take care of them no matter how she felt.

"Please stop crying," Libby said weakly as she held their hands. They stopped crying as they walked the two blocks to their house. Tears pricked Libby's eyes, but she blinked them away before the kids saw them.

At the Mason house Lori slammed the door hard, rattling the glass in it. Her face was brick red, and anger shot from her dark eyes. "I hate those girls!"

"No, Lori," said Libby, shaking her head. She wanted to hate them too, but she knew it wasn't right. "Jesus says to love others."

"Well, I won't!" Lori crossed her arms over her thin chest, stamped her foot, and stuck out her chin. "So, there!"

Pete looked at Lori then copied her.

Libby sighed heavily. She wanted to go home, but she knew she had to stay with the kids until Bill got home and Chuck came to pick her up. "Let's sit down and talk," said Libby. She knew it wouldn't do any good to yell at the kids, so she decided to try talking like Chuck always did with her.

Suddenly Lori turned and kicked Libby in the shin. "I won't sit down! I won't talk!"

Libby yelped and danced around on one leg while holding the other. "Don't do that again, Lori! I mean it!"

"You're being bad, Lori," said Pete. "You promised Dad you wouldn't be bad again!"

Lori pushed Pete, and he fell to the floor with a plop. He burst into tears.

Libby gathered him in her arms and sat on the rocker with him. She watched Lori run to the bedroom. Libby brushed Pete's blond hair back and kissed his forehead. All her life she'd wanted someone to do that to her. Now that she lived with a family that would, she was too old. "You're OK, Pete. Stop crying."

Pete snuggled against Libby and sucked his thumb, whimpering now and then.

Libby rocked Pete but couldn't think of anything to say.

Suddenly Pete sat up. "I want to watch cartoons."

"Go ahead," Libby said with a small laugh. She'd

thought Pete would cry for hours. "I'll go check on Lori."

"She's probably hiding under the bed," said Pete as he clicked on the TV.

Libby frowned as she walked to the small bedroom. She stopped just inside the door and looked at the bunk beds. Lori wasn't on the top bunk where she slept, and she wasn't on the bottom where Pete slept.

"Lori, I want to talk to you," Libby said softly. She listened, but couldn't hear a sound. Finally she got down on her hands and knees and looked under the bed. Lori was huddled in a corner with a stuffed rabbit in her arms and two dirty socks balled up beside her. Dust balls lay in the places Lori hadn't been.

"Get away," said Lori hoarsely.

"Please come out and talk to me," said Libby softly.

"No!"

"Then I'll come talk to you." Libby slid on her back under the bed. Dust tickled her nose, and she almost sneezed. The sheeting on the springs was partly ripped, exposing springs and batting.

"I won't talk," whispered Lori.

"I know you feel terrible about kicking me and pushing Pete," said Libby. "I know you want to tell us you're sorry, but sometimes it's hard to do."

"It is," Lori said weakly as she hugged the stuffed rabbit close.

"Pete knows you're sorry, but he wants you to tell him just to make sure," said Libby. She saw a smear of dust on Lori's cheek and another on her blouse and jeans.

"I am sorry," said Lori with a sniff.

"I forgive you," said Libby. It had taken her a long time to learn to forgive, but with help from Jesus, she had. "So will Pete."

"Those two girls were mean," said Lori, looking up at the bed springs.

"Can we sit on the bed and talk?" asked Libby. "It's dusty under here, and my nose tickles."

Lori nodded.

Libby scooted out from under the bed and waited for Lori. Libby brushed dust off herself and off Lori; then they sat on the edge of the bottom bunk. Libby took Lori's small hand in hers. "Those girls were mean. I'm sorry they hurt you and Pete."

Lori looked ready to cry again. "I hate them!"

Libby shook her head. "Jesus says to love even those who hurt you. I know you want to do what Jesus wants you to do." The words stung Libby. She wanted to do what Jesus wanted also, but she didn't always do it. She felt the unicorn in her pocket and felt even worse.

Lori's lip quivered. "Will Dad really have to go back to jail?"

"No!"

"But they said he stole a unicorn."

"He says he didn't," said Libby. "And I believe him."

"I'm so scared he'll leave us again and go back to prison! Pete and I don't want to live without him again! I wish we were happy and never had to worry about Dad leaving us!"

Libby touched the unicorn. Could she make Lori's wish on the lucky unicorn? Suddenly Libby realized how useless it was. It couldn't really help her or Lori. Only Jesus could. The unicorn was make-believe. Jesus was real.

"I'm so scared, Libby!" Lori flung her arms around Libby and buried her face in Libby's neck.

Remembering all the times she'd been afraid, Libby held Lori tightly. "Lori, fear comes from Satan, and he's our enemy. God gave us the spirit of power and love and a sound mind. You don't have to be afraid. Say, 'Satan, in the name of Jesus, you get away from me with your fear! I am full of God's power and love and sound mind!'"

Lori nodded hard. "Dad says Satan is bad and tries to do bad things to us. I won't let Satan make me be afraid that Dad's going back to prison! I will trust God to take care of us!"

Libby nodded. How could she have let herself believe the unicorn brought her good luck? The unicorn was only a piece of jewelry and couldn't help her at all! Her heavenly Father was her helper! He would even help her return the unicorn!

TEN
Brenda Wilkens

After supper Libby stood in the pen beside the horse barn and slowly brushed Snowball, her horse. Libby's brain whirled with ways to return the unicorn on Friday. She couldn't just walk into the office and explain what she'd done. It would cause too much trouble for her and even for Susan because she'd kept the secret.

Just then Susan walked to the fence and leaned against it. "You've sure been quiet since you got home, Libby. Were Lori and Pete hard to baby-sit today?"

"I had some trouble," said Libby. She patted Snowball then walked to the fence and leaned against it, the brush in her hand. Snowball strolled over to the tank and drank the cold water. A warm breeze blew Libby's hair away from her flushed cheek as she told

Susan what had happened with Lori and Pete. "I've decided to return the unicorn tomorrow."

"That's great!" Susan sighed loudly. "It's been a hard secret to keep!"

"I don't know if I ever want to see another unicorn," said Libby.

"What about a unicorn?" asked Brenda Wilkens as she walked up. She wore new jeans and a lavender blouse tucked in at her narrow waist.

Libby's heart zoomed to her feet. Had Brenda heard everything? "I didn't know you were here, Brenda."

"I just got here," said Brenda. She ignored Susan and glared at Libby. "Gabby called me and told me how mean you were in the park."

"Mean?" Libby cried in shock. "Gabby and Nedra were mean! They made Lori and Pete cry."

"I'm going to tell everyone on the bus in the morning that you stole the unicorn, Libby Dobbs," said Brenda. "And when I get to school, I'll tell Mr. Gavin!"

Libby's heart turned over.

"Don't do it, Brenda," said Susan sharply. "You don't want to make trouble for Libby again. You know what your dad said."

Brenda shrugged. "He won't really do anything. Besides, Libby hurt my friends, so I'll hurt her. She deserves it."

"She does not!" cried Susan.

Blood pounded in Libby's ears. She wanted to throw the brush at Brenda, but she didn't. Would she ever get away from Brenda Wilkens's hatred? Brenda had no idea the trouble she'd cause if she told that story! Libby gripped the top rail of the fence. She had to turn in the unicorn before Brenda had a chance to spread her story. Libby bit back a groan. Oh, why hadn't she left the unicorn on the bathroom shelf! Or better yet, why hadn't she turned it in at the office when she'd first found it?

"You look scared to death, Libby," said Brenda with a cruel laugh. "Are you guilty? You look like it. Is that it? You really did help Bill Mason steal the unicorn!"

"That's not true!" cried Libby.

"Libby doesn't steal," said Susan firmly.

"How do you know, Susan?" asked Brenda coldly.

Susan pushed her face right up to Brenda's. "Go home where you belong!"

Brenda flushed but didn't back down. "I came to see Ben, and I'll see him if I want! You can't make me leave."

Libby wanted to leap over the fence and punch Brenda, but she knew Jesus didn't want her to. She stood very still and watched Brenda run toward the field where Ben was playing ball with Kevin and Toby. "What will I do, Susan?"

"Tell Dad everything."

Libby's stomach knotted. "I can't! I just can't!" She didn't want Chuck to hate her.

"Oh, Libby," said Susan sadly. "Do you want me to tell since you can't?"

"No!" Libby leaped over the fence and gripped Susan's arm. "You promised!"

"I won't tell," Susan said.

Libby breathed easier as she stepped away from Susan. "I'll turn in the unicorn in the morning." She considered telling Susan she'd overheard Mr. Gavin say the unicorn in the museum was the fake one, but if she did, Susan wouldn't be able to keep the secret that her unicorn was worth a fortune.

"I'm glad you're going to turn it in," said Susan.

"I have to practice piano now," said Libby.

"I wish I didn't have to baby-sit Jake and Al tonight," said Susan as she fell into step beside Libby.

"I didn't know you had to."

"Yes, Mrs. Grant called just before you got home and asked if I could. She said she'd pick me up before eight."

"Take along a game and a video like you did the last time," said Libby.

"I will, but I still don't want to go. Sometimes I

think I'll quit baby-sitting. It is a way to earn money, but it's hard work!" Susan suddenly laughed. "Libby, you go baby-sit the boys!"

"Me? But I already baby-sat Lori and Pete today. And I have to practice piano and study for a science test."

A stubborn look on her face, Susan stopped near the picnic table. Goosy Poosy honked, and Rex barked at the boys. Susan stood with her hands at her waist and her feet apart. "I don't want to baby-sit! I'll make a deal with you, Libby."

"What?" asked Libby hesitantly. She didn't like the look on Susan's face.

"You baby-sit for me tonight, and I won't tell your secret."

Libby gasped. Did Susan really know what she was doing? "Susan, I can't even believe you're doing this to me! That's blackmail!"

Susan hunched her shoulders. "I know, but I'm desperate."

"I can't believe you!"

Susan wrinkled her nose. "You baby-sit for me, and I'll keep your secret."

A shiver trickled down Libby's spine. "You wouldn't really tell, would you?"

Susan shrugged. "I wouldn't want to, but I might if

I have to baby-sit those boys again. I just can't stand to do it, Libby! I can't!"

"Oh, all right! But you have to see if it's all right with Mrs. Grant and with Mom."

Susan looked guilty, but she didn't back down. "I'm sure they'll agree."

An hour later Libby walked beside Mrs. Grant to the back door of her house. Libby wanted to tell Mrs. Grant to take her home, but she knew she had to baby-sit even though she didn't want to.

"We'll be gone only an hour or two," said Mrs. Grant. "The boys must be in bed before ten."

Libby nodded. She had one of Toby's games and a video Toby and Kevin especially liked. She'd left the unicorn at home in her puzzle box. For once she'd hidden her puzzle box under a few stuffed animals in a wicker basket beside her round red hassock. She didn't want to take a chance on Toby or Kevin finding the directions and opening her box. It would be terrible if Chuck and Vera learned about the unicorn. They'd never believe or trust her again. They might even send her away.

Libby walked into the living room and saw Al and Jake watching TV and Mr. Grant reading the newspaper. Feeling awkward, Libby stopped beside an overstuffed chair.

"We're back," said Mrs. Grant.

Mr. Grant dropped the paper in a basket beside the couch. "Hi, Libby." He jumped up and turned to the boys. "Libby's here, boys."

"Libby!" they cried then punched each other and laughed.

Libby trembled. Would the boys be naughty again?

"You boys be good for Libby," said Mrs. Grant. "There are potato chips in the cupboard and dip in the refrigerator. Bed before ten, boys, without any trouble."

The boys groaned but didn't argue. They looked at Libby and grinned. She knew just what they were thinking, and she wanted to leave.

"I hope the board meeting doesn't last long," said Mr. Grant as he lifted his jacket from the closet.

"Mr. Gavin is certainly out to make trouble for poor Bill Mason," said Mrs. Grant as they walked out the door.

"The man could be guilty," said Mr. Grant as he closed the door after them.

An icy chill ran down Libby's back. Could Mr. Gavin make the school board dismiss Bill Mason? What would he do if he lost his job? How would he feed his kids or keep his house? It would be terrible if Pete and Lori were taken away from their dad and put in a foster home.

Suddenly a throw pillow struck Libby in the head.

The rain in spain
stays mainly in the
plain.

——————— that
side

→

How many books I have done on a piece of paper. 1,

She jumped and bit back a scream. She wanted to grab the boys and shake them, but instead she held up the game and said, "You guys might be too young to play this, but Toby said you might like it." Libby knew the boys would want to play just to prove they could do it.

"We can play it!" they shouted as they ran to the kitchen after Libby to set it up.

Libby forced her thoughts off of Bill Mason and onto the game with the boys.

They played two games and watched the video without causing any trouble. Before ten Libby put them to bed, talked to them a while then walked back to the living room. Did Bill know the school board was meeting tonight to discuss him? Why was Mr. Gavin so determined to blame Bill for the robbery?

Libby sank to the couch and locked her hands over her knees. The phone rang, and she almost jumped out of her skin. She hated answering the phone when she baby-sat. She never knew what to say. Reluctantly she picked up the phone on the end table and said, "Hello."

"Libby, it's Susan."

Libby scowled. "What do you want?"

Susan didn't say anything for a long time. "I feel really bad for what I did to you."

Her eyes wide in alarm, Libby leaned forward. "Did you tell about the unicorn?"

"No! I feel bad for forcing you to baby-sit tonight. It was wrong of me, and I couldn't stand it any longer so I called to apologize. I was afraid I'd already be asleep when you got home. I'm sorry, Libby. Please, please, please forgive me!"

Slowly Libby leaned back on the couch. Should she forgive Susan or make her worry all night long?

"Please, Libby," said Susan, sounding close to tears.

Libby smiled. "I forgive you, Susan."

"Oh, good! How's it been tonight?"

"We played a game, and the boys watched a video while I studied my science, so it's been all right."

"I'm glad. I'd hate it if they'd been naughty."

"Susan, did you know the school board is meeting with Mr. Gavin tonight to talk about Bill Mason?" asked Libby.

"Mrs. Grant said they were going to a school board meeting, but I didn't know why. Oh, Libby, I hope they don't force Bill to quit!"

"Me, too." Libby twisted the white cord on the phone.

"We'll pray everything works out right for Bill," said Susan.

"Good idea," said Libby. Would she ever remember to pray about the problems instead of just talking about them or worrying about them?

When she hung up, Libby whispered, "Heavenly Father, take care of Bill and his kids. Stop Mr. Gavin from hurting Bill. In Jesus' name. Amen."

Libby smiled. God answered prayer. He'd help Bill Mason, and he'd even help her return the unicorn.

"Maybe I can slip the unicorn into the gold exhibit and let someone else find it," whispered Libby. She frowned. Would that be right to do? Oh, sometimes it was very hard to do the right thing!

ELEVEN
Brenda's lie

Libby finished her last bite of oatmeal, wiped her mouth, then carried her bowl to the sink. Already the day was starting out wrong—oatmeal for breakfast. She liked oatmeal, but she'd wanted cold cereal this morning.

Vera looked up from pouring herself another cup of tea from the flowered china teapot. "The Scripture for today is Psalm 46:1, 'God is our refuge and strength, a very present help in trouble.'"

Libby shot a look at Susan. Had she told? But Susan looked innocent, and Libby relaxed.

Just then Toby dropped a small ball, and it bounced across the kitchen. He ran after it and finally cornered it and picked it up.

Kevin grabbed the ball from Toby. "That's my little blue ball! You can't take that to school!"

"It's not yours," cried Toby, his face as red as his hair. "I found it at school yesterday."

Kevin looked at it closer. "I guess it's not mine. It doesn't have a black mark on it like mine does. Sorry, Toby."

Vera took it from Kevin and looked sternly at Toby. "Tell me about the ball."

Her stomach knotted, Libby stood back, the unicorn tucked safely in the pocket of her jeans.

Toby looked ready to cry. "I found it in the playground! Nobody wanted it. It's only a cheap little ball."

Vera slipped her arm around Toby. "It's not your ball, Toby. If it only cost a penny or if it cost a thousand dollars, it's still not yours to keep. You must turn it in. If no one claims it, then you can have it. But you can't just take it. That's stealing."

Chills ran down Libby's spine. What would Vera say if she knew about the $4,000 unicorn in her pocket? Libby bit her lip. Taking the unicorn even for luck had been stealing even though she'd tried to tell herself it wasn't. Silently she said, "Heavenly Father, forgive me for stealing. I'm sorry and I won't do it again."

Toby twisted the toe of his sneaker on the floor. "I'm sorry, Mom. I'll take it to the office."

"Good," said Vera.

"But the kids will laugh at me," said Toby.

"Even if they laugh, you must turn the ball in," said Vera.

Toby sighed. "I will. But it won't be easy."

Libby knew exactly how he felt.

"Your heavenly Father will help you," said Vera softly. She kissed Toby. "He's your refuge, your strength, and your help."

Toby nodded.

Libby did, too. She dared not forget that, or she'd never be able to return the unicorn. She glanced up to find Susan looking at her, and she turned away quickly before Vera saw the look and read the thoughts on her face.

A few minutes later Libby reluctantly followed Susan onto the school bus. She steeled herself for Brenda's nasty remarks, but none came. Libby looked at the kids on the bus but couldn't see Brenda.

"Hey, Joe, where's Brenda?" Susan asked.

Joe shrugged as Ben sat beside him. "She rode to town with Mom."

Libby sagged in the seat in relief with Susan beside her. Brenda wasn't on the bus to tell her lies, and she wouldn't be in school to tell them. By Monday nobody would be interested in hearing about the unicorn.

"I'm glad she's not here," whispered Susan as the bus started forward with a lurch.

"Me, too!" Libby smiled. Maybe it wasn't going to be as bad a day as she'd thought.

Later at school Libby walked to the office. She took a deep breath then another one. She silently thanked God for helping her and for giving her strength to do what was right.

Several kids stood at the tall desk and waited for Miss Richie to finish talking on the phone. Libby stood on one foot then the other while she waited her turn. Ice flowed in her veins, and she almost ran from the office. Finally Miss Richie looked at Libby.

"Miss Richie," said Libby. She swallowed and couldn't say another word.

"What is it, Libby?" asked Miss Richie impatiently.

"It's about . . . the . . . unicorn." Libby could hardly breathe. "I have it."

Miss Richie scowled. "You get out of here Libby Dobbs! That's not a bit funny!"

Libby held out her hand with the unicorn in it, but Miss Richie wouldn't even look.

"I don't have time for jokes! You get to class right now!"

"But what about this unicorn?" asked Libby weakly.

"Mr. Gavin was just on the phone to me, and he said everything was fine at the exhibit. He said he was happy to report the unicorn was right where it belonged." Miss Richie shook her finger at Libby. "Now, get out of here and let me get to work!"

"I'll go see Mr. Page then."

"You'll do no such thing! He's too busy for jokes!" Miss Richie frowned impatiently. "Now, get to class!"

Libby pushed the unicorn back into her pocket and slowly walked into the hallway crowded with clamoring boys and girls. Libby's head spun, and she leaned weakly against the wall near the library door. Why wouldn't Miss Richie at least look at the unicorn? And why would Mr. Gavin say the unicorn was right where it belonged when he knew it wasn't the real one?

Just then Timmy jabbed Libby's arm. Libby jumped so hard she almost fell over.

"Brenda told everybody you helped Bill Mason steal the unicorn," said Timmy.

"I thought she wasn't coming to school today."

"She did." Timmy peered into Libby's pale face. "Is it true?"

Libby's legs almost gave way. She helplessly shook her head. "You know it's not true!"

"Mr. Gavin asked a bunch of us about it," said Timmy. "So I told him about the white box and that you have it."

Libby's head spun. What was happening? Chuck had the box, and he'd talked with Dave Knotts about it, but so far the police hadn't done any investigating. "What did Mr. Gavin say when you told him that?" asked Libby hoarsely.

"He said he wanted to talk to you right away," said Timmy. "I didn't want to come to school today, but I'm glad I did."

Several girls walked past and looked at Libby suspiciously.

"Do they all think I'm guilty?" Libby asked.

Timmy shrugged. "Who knows? Most of them don't know you very well. But they know Brenda, and they might believe what she says."

"It's not fair! Brenda is lying!" Libby stopped short. She did have the unicorn, so she couldn't say Brenda was telling a total lie. "I'm going to talk to Bill Mason."

"I saw him talking with the head janitor a while ago near the furnace room," said Timmy.

"Thanks, Timmy!" Libby ran down the crowded hall toward the furnace room. She heard someone call to her, but she kept running. Maybe Bill would know what she should do.

She stopped outside the closed door, knocked, then peeked inside. She saw the furnace and the janitor's big desk. Nobody was there. "I need your help real bad, Jesus," whispered Libby as she touched the unicorn.

She turned and walked slowly back the way she'd come. She'd have to get to math class before she was marked tardy. Just then she spotted Mr. Gavin talking to Susan. Libby's heart dropped to her feet. She didn't want to talk to Mr. Gavin yet. Frantically she looked around, dashed to the girls' rest room then leaned against a sink with her head down.

Just then Susan's friend Jamie Smith stepped from a stall. "Libby, what's wrong?"

"I can't tell you," whispered Libby.

"Is it about the unicorn?" asked Jamie softly. She was a head shorter than Libby and just as thin.

Libby nodded.

"I don't believe you stole it or helped Bill Mason steal it," said Jamie. "Other kids feel the same way."

"Thanks," said Libby. "I wanted to talk to Bill, but I can't find him."

"I saw him going out the back door just before I came in here," said Jamie.

"I'll see if he's still there." Libby pushed open the door and cautiously peered out. She couldn't see Mr. Gavin at all. She glanced back at Jamie and whispered, "See you later."

Jamie nodded and smiled.

Libby ran to the back door and stepped outdoors. The warm breeze ruffled her hair and cooled off her warm face. She looked past the yard to the football field. She couldn't see Bill anywhere. Just then a movement at the corner of the building caught her attention. Bill and Mr. Gavin were standing together talking in hushed tones. Libby trembled. Was Mr. Gavin accusing Bill of stealing the unicorn? Bill didn't look upset at all. Mr. Gavin reached in his pocket and pulled out some money. He handed some to Bill, and Bill stuck it in his pocket.

Her heart racing, Libby slipped back inside. What did it mean? Were Bill and Mr. Gavin working together? Libby remembered Chuck had told her that as a Christian she was led by the spirit of God and she'd know who to trust. "I need to know if I should trust Bill and Mr. Gavin, heavenly Father," whispered Libby. "Help me know, and help me know what to do next."

Maybe she shouldn't trust either of them right now. She should take the unicorn to Mr. Page and tell him everything. But what if she couldn't trust him either?

Sweat popped out on Libby's forehead as she slowly walked down the empty hallway. Her sneakers were quiet on the tile floor. She'd go to math class, and after that maybe she'd know what to do. The unicorn felt heavy in her pocket as she walked toward the classroom.

TWELVE
Mr. Gavin

After math class Libby walked reluctantly into the hallway behind Susan. Smells of perfume and hair gel drifted out from the passing students.

"Mr. Gavin was asking about you, Libby," whispered Susan.

Libby glanced around, but saw only the noisy sixth graders. "I saw him talking to you. What did he want?"

"He said he wanted to tell you the unicorn is back in place, and he's not going to press charges against Bill since he doesn't have enough proof."

"Do you believe him?" asked Libby.

Susan shrugged.

"Did he hear the lies Brenda spread around?"

"Yes."

"I hope he doesn't believe them," whispered Libby.

102

Slowly she walked with Susan toward English class. The unicorn seemed to get heavier and heavier. Maybe she should call Chuck and tell him everything and let him take care of it. She shook her head. She didn't want Chuck to know what a terrible thing she'd done.

Libby followed Susan into English class then stopped short when she saw Mr. Gavin talking to the teacher. Should she get permission to speak with him and give him the unicorn?

Mr. Gavin looked up and spotted Libby. "There she is now. I appreciate your letting me take her from class."

Libby shivered, her muscles tensed and ready for flight. She just couldn't bring herself to trust Mr. Gavin enough to give him the unicorn in her pocket. Maybe he was the one who'd tried to frame Bill.

"Libby, shall we step out into the hallway, please?" asked Mr. Gavin with a smile that didn't reach his eyes.

Libby trembled.

"Shall I come with you?" whispered Susan.

"That won't be necessary," said Mr. Gavin as he gripped Libby's arm and ushered her out the door and into the quiet hallway just as the tardy bell rang.

"Why do you want me?" asked Libby weakly.

"To let you know I heard the rumors about your

helping Mason steal the unicorn." Mr. Gavin flipped back his dark suit jacket and rested his hands on his hips. "I understand you had the unicorn with you Monday during the day and took it to your home then gave it to Mason Tuesday."

"No! That's not true!" Libby knew Gabby had had the unicorn Monday and brought it back Tuesday when she'd found it in the rest room. Libby's brain whirled but then clicked sharply into what had happened. Tuesday Susan had brought home the other unicorn, so Tuesday night both were at their house. Libby looked closely at Mr. Gavin. "Our class went to the exhibit Tuesday. I was sure the unicorn was there."

Mr. Gavin nodded. "So it was. But how is it someone saw you with it Monday?"

"Someone lied," said Libby, her mouth bone dry.

"I want to believe it was a prank. We have the unicorn back safely, but I want the thief punished."

Libby wanted to shout at him and ask why he wasn't doing anything about the fake unicorn, but she kept quiet for fear he was the thief.

Mr. Gavin smiled slightly. "After we leave here today we'll take the unicorn to the museum and leave it there where no one can touch it. It can't be stolen from there."

Libby moved restlessly. Why was he doing that?

Wasn't he going to tell anyone he had a forged unicorn? "Will you try to get the other charms to the set?" asked Libby, watching Mr. Gavin closely for his reaction.

He grew very still. "What other charms?"

"Bill told us about the four charms Josef Mueller crafted for his daughters."

"Oh, that! I heard it was only speculation, not reality."

"Oh," said Libby, but she didn't believe him. "Bill said the collection together would be priceless. He said someone could make a copy of the charms and leave the real ones in the museum and no one would ever know it."

"I hope that's not what Mason plans to do," said Mr. Gavin coldly.

"He won't. He said even when he was a thief it was out of his league." Libby wanted to clamp her mouth shut, but she wanted even more to learn if Mr. Gavin was guilty of making the copy and stealing the original. He had to have a very good reason for not telling everyone about the fake unicorn.

Just then Mr. Page and Bill Mason walked toward them, and a brilliant idea popped into Libby's head. It frightened her so badly she didn't know if she could carry it out. Silently she asked God to show her exactly what to do and say.

106

"Mr. Page, Bill," Libby said. "I need to talk to you both."

Mr. Page stopped beside them. "Hello, Libby. Mr. Gavin," Mr. Page said with a nod.

"Gavin," said Bill Mason before he turned to Libby with a smile.

"Mason," said Mr. Gavin with a nod.

Libby suddenly remembered seeing Mr. Gavin giving money to Bill, and she almost backed out of her plan.

Mr. Gavin rattled change and keys in his pocket. "I'd better get back to the exhibit. I told my assistant he'd have to do only one narration for me."

"Wait," said Libby. "Mr. Page, have you heard about Josef Mueller's collection?"

"Yes," said Mr. Page.

"What if the unicorn in the exhibit is a copy?" said Libby.

"It's not," snapped Mr. Gavin.

Mr. Page whistled in shock. "That would be quite a blow. I'd feel a lot better if I knew it wasn't," said Mr. Page. "I don't want this school responsible for such a switch. How can we learn the truth, Mr. Gavin?"

"Nitric acid." Libby said quickly. The others looked at her strangely. "My dad told me," Libby added awkwardly.

Bill smiled and nodded. "I could get some from the lab."

"They don't have any," said Libby then suddenly realized she might have given herself away. "I was going to do an experiment and asked Mr. Marston about it one day," she said quickly.

"The high school might have some," said Mr. Page. "The jewelry store would have some for sure."

"I refuse to go to such bother!" snapped Mr. Gavin. "I've already tested it on my own."

"I'd feel a lot better to witness the test," said Mr. Page.

Libby knew once Mr. Page wanted something done, he'd see it got done. He was very stubborn.

"I'll get the nitric acid." Bill smiled at Libby again then strode away, his rubber-soled shoes soundless on the tile.

Suddenly Mr. Page turned to Libby. "What's this about taking a unicorn to the office as a joke this morning?"

Libby's hands turned icy cold.

"What unicorn?" asked Mr. Gavin sharply.

"It was nothing, Mr. Gavin," said Mr. Page. "But after this, young lady, you keep your jokes at home."

Libby nodded weakly. She didn't dare look at Mr. Gavin. Her fingers itched to touch the unicorn, but she pushed her hair behind her ear instead.

"You get back to class now, Libby," said Mr. Page. "Mr. Gavin, you and I will go to the exhibit and wait for Bill."

Mr. Gavin cleared his throat. "You go ahead. I'll be right there."

As Mr. Page walked away, Libby started for the classroom door. Suddenly Mr. Gavin gripped her arm and blocked the door. Startled, she looked at him. His face was dark with anger.

"I want that other unicorn," Mr. Gavin growled.

Libby twisted free and leaped away then ran down the hall, fear pricking her skin.

THIRTEEN
The closet

Fearfully Libby glanced back and saw Mr. Gavin running after her. His feet were loud on the floor. She tried to scream for help, but she couldn't force even a low sound out. Suddenly she thought about running into a classroom. Mr. Gavin would never dare burst in after her. She swerved to the first door and grabbed the knob. It wouldn't turn! She looked over her shoulder to find Mr. Gavin almost on her. She ran across the hall and grasped the knob. It turned easily, and she opened the door just as Mr. Gavin grabbed for her. She felt his touch just as she jumped inside the room. It was Mr. Marston's early science class. He looked up with an angry frown. The class turned, stared at Libby, and laughed. The room seemed closed in and hot.

"What's going on, Libby?" Mr. Marston asked gruffly as he stood.

Libby gasped for breath, her face damp and her chest rising and falling with fear. She wanted to tell Mr. Marston what was happening, but the words were locked inside her.

"Have you been racing in the hall?" Mr. Marston asked as he strode toward her while the class laughed louder.

Libby fell back a step, frightened of his anger. Again she tried to speak, but no sound came out.

"I've warned you students about having races in the hall!" Mr. Marston gripped Libby's arm. "You march right to Mr. Page's office this instant."

Libby struggled to pull free, but Mr. Marston's grip was too tight. She couldn't let him put her out in the hall where Mr. Gavin was waiting to grab her!

The students whispered and giggled. Libby tried to ask them for help, but she couldn't.

Mr. Marston jerked open the door and pushed Libby out.

Frantically Libby looked around for Mr. Gavin, but he wasn't in sight. Maybe she could get to Mr. Page's office before Mr. Gavin could catch her.

"You report to the office. I'll be in later to give them my complaint." Mr. Marston closed the door with a final click that seemed to ring down the empty hallway.

Shivers ran up and down Libby's back as she looked down the hall. She had to go only a few more feet, turn left at the corner, and the office was at the end of the hall. If she turned right, she'd go to the cafeteria. Was Mr. Gavin standing just around the corner waiting for her?

Slowly, cautiously, Libby crept to the corner. Her jeans and blouse felt too hot and tight. The smell of food from the cafeteria turned her stomach. She stopped and listened. Was that someone breathing? Dare she peek around? Finally she inched ahead then peeked around the corner just in time to see Mr. Gavin slip into the boys' rest room. It was between her and the office! She dared not run that way. She looked the other way. The janitor's closet door was open slightly. She could hide in there until Mr. Gavin gave up and stopped looking for her. Bill would be back soon, and he'd look for Mr. Gavin until he found him to be in on the testing of the unicorn.

Libby eased around the corner and ran quietly to the closet. A picture of Mother locking her in a closet flashed across her mind. Fear gripped her, and she couldn't slip inside. Her heart pounded so loudly she was afraid Mr. Gavin could hear it. She couldn't just stand in the hallway and get caught! She heard the rattle of pots and pans and the sound of voices from the kitchen. Could she go to them for help? She shook her head. She couldn't take a chance.

Taking a shuddering breath, Libby slipped into the closet. She'd leave the door open a crack then she'd be all right. Dust tickled her nose. Water dripped in the large sink. The smell of cleaning supplies almost choked her.

Just then she heard footsteps walking down the hall. They were loud like Mr. Gavin's. Libby pressed her hand to her heart and waited. The person walked past, and Libby could see through the crack in the door that it was Mr. Gavin. She covered her mouth to keep from whimpering in fear. He walked out of sight, and finally his footsteps faded away, but she knew he'd be back. She'd have to shut the door. But he'd probably try the door and look inside. She'd be trapped!

Her brain whirled and she felt dizzy as she realized she'd have to lock herself in. Could she do it?

She inched open the door just enough to reach around and turn the lock. It could be locked by turning the lock but only unlocked with a key. Could she stand to be locked in? Stinging tears burned her eyes as she clicked the lock with a trembling hand.

"I got you now, Libby!" hissed Mr. Gavin as he reached for her, his hand brushing hers.

With all the strength in her she pulled the door hard. It closed with a loud snap.

Mr. Gavin rattled the knob then rapped on the door. "You can't get away from me that easily. I'll get Mason to come get you out."

Libby fell back from the door and whimpered.

"Don't think Bill Mason will help you. He's working with me. You have no one to help you! No one will believe you."

A giant tear rolled down Libby's cheek. Was Bill Mason really in on the theft? Was Mr. Gavin lying just to frighten her even more?

"You will be sorry for this, girl," hissed Mr. Gavin with one last rattle of the doorknob. "I'll have you sent to a reform school where you'll stay forever!"

Libby stood glued to the middle of the floor for a long time. The silence stretched on and on. She heard footsteps, but she didn't dare knock or call out. Mr. Gavin would grab her and convince the others that he was taking her to Mr. Page.

The darkness pressed against her, and she fumbled around until she found the light switch. The light filled the room, blinding her for a while.

She struggled for breath. Blood pounded in her ears. She was locked in just as she had been many times in the past! She had to get out now! She couldn't stay locked in a second longer! She doubled her fists to pound on the door. No, she couldn't take the chance. Slowly she opened her hands and spread them across the door and leaned her forehead against one hand.

From the past Mother's angry voice floated to her. "Libby Dobbs, you are a very naughty girl! You can't come out until you promise to be good."

"I'll be good, Mother! I will, I will!"

"You don't mean it, Libby. I won't let you out."

"Let me out! Mother, let me out! Please! Please!"

Libby shook her head and forced back the terrible memories. Tears slipped down her ashen cheeks. Weakly she sank to the floor and huddled against the door, her hands over her face.

Suddenly from deep inside her she heard, "Libby, I am always with you. Do not fear. I am your refuge and strength, a very present help in trouble."

Libby lifted her head, her eyes wide. She remembered the Scripture Vera had given them for the day. Libby smiled weakly. "Heavenly Father, you are always with me!" she whispered in awe. "You are my refuge and strength and my help when I'm in trouble! I don't have to be afraid even inside a locked closet! Thank you, Father God! Thank you!"

Libby wiped away her tears as she continued to talk to God. She'd never thought she could be free of the fear of being locked in a closet, but she felt the fear slip away.

Just then she heard footsteps. Slowly she stood, her heart racing. Was it Bill Mason coming to unlock the door? She trembled. Could she trust Bill after what Mr. Gavin had said.

A key grated in the lock. Libby stood with her fingers laced together and her eyes glued to the doorknob.

FOURTEEN
The secret of the unicorns

Libby bit back a scream as she watched the closet
door open. Sam, the head janitor, stood there. He
was almost as old as Grandpa Johnson, and he had a
bald head. Sam jumped when he saw Libby.

"What are you doing in here?" Sam asked sharply.

"I'm in trouble," Libby said weakly as she tried to
peek around Sam. "I need to find Mr. Page right now.
Will you take me to him? Please?"

Sam frowned but nodded. "You sure look like you
need help."

"I do. Mr. Gavin from the museum is trying to hurt
me." Libby shivered just thinking about what he'd do
to her if he found her.

Sam shook his head as he rubbed the front of his
overalls. "Now, why would he do that?"

"Take me to Mr. Page so I can tell him," said Libby

as she darted a look around. Was Mr. Gavin hiding nearby to grab her, or was he in the trailer with the exhibit?

"I don't have time to take you to the office," said Sam. "I got a stopped-up toilet to take care of before it floods the boys' rest room."

Libby bit her lower lip. Silently she prayed for the Lord to show her what to do. Mr. Gavin wasn't in sight, so she could run as fast as she could to the office then from there go to the exhibit.

Sam took a plunger from the closet and left the door ajar. "You run on to the office, and let me get my work done," he said.

Libby nodded, but she stayed beside him as he walked toward the boys' rest room, the very one Mr. Gavin had slipped into a while ago.

Libby's stomach knotted as Sam reached the rest room door. It didn't open and Mr. Gavin didn't leap out and grab her. She breathed a sigh of relief then sped down the hall toward the office. She burst through the door and stopped short. Mr. Gavin was talking with Miss Richie! He turned and saw her, and his eyes narrowed into slits of steel.

"Where's Mr. Page?" asked Libby frantically.

"In the museum exhibit," said Miss Richie.

"And that's just where we're going now," said Mr.

Gavin. He stepped toward her, but she turned and fled, slamming the office door behind her.

She raced out the front door into the bright spring day. A minibus waited at the curb. She glanced behind her to see Mr. Gavin running after her. She sped past the bus and down the walk to the side of the building. She heard Mr. Gavin behind her, and she ran faster. She rounded the corner and darted up the steps and into the exhibit.

Mr. Page, Bill, and Mr. Gavin's assistant stood together near the display where the unicorn was.

"What kept you, Libby?" asked Mr. Page coldly.

Libby opened her mouth to answer, but Mr. Gavin stepped past her.

"She was trying to get away, and I stopped her," said Mr. Gavin. "I finally have the whole thing figured out. She helped Mason take the real unicorn from the display and replace it with a fake. If you check the one on display you'll find it's a copy."

Libby stared in horror at Mr. Gavin then looked helplessly at Bill Mason. Who would believe either of them?

His face bleak, Bill shook his head. "That's a lie! I didn't steal the unicorn, and neither did Libby."

Libby flushed. That wasn't exactly true. She'd had the unicorn since Tuesday. "Mr. Gavin tried to hurt me," she said, but she didn't sound very convincing. "He stole the unicorn and is trying to blame us."

Mr. Gavin laughed and shook his head. "That's ridiculous!" There was a sound at the door, and Libby looked up. It was Chuck! Joy burst inside her, and she cried, "Dad! I'm so glad you're here!"

"Bill called me," said Chuck as he strode to Libby and placed his hand on her shoulder. "He said you'd need me."

"I do," Libby whispered.

Chuck looked at the others. "What's going on here?"

"Your daughter and Mason have stolen the unicorn," said Mr. Gavin.

"Impossible," said Chuck. He peered through the glass case at the unicorn. "It's right there."

"And I have the other one," said Libby, pulling the unicorn from her pocket. She felt as if a thousand pounds had lifted off her back.

The others gasped as Chuck took the unicorn, studying Libby closely. "How did you get this?" he asked softly.

"She stole it!" snapped Mr. Gavin.

"I didn't!" cried Libby.

"Tell us what happened," said Chuck.

"It'll be lies," growled Mr. Gavin.

"Let her talk," said Mr. Page.

Holding tightly to Chuck's hand, Libby told her story. She ended with Mr. Gavin chasing her to get the unicorn from her.

"I have every right to it!" Mr. Gavin cried.

"We'll test both unicorns and see what we have," said Mr. Page. He turned to the assistant. "Will you do it, Cam?"

"I'll do it," said Mr. Gavin coldly.

"I prefer to have Cam do it," said Mr. Page. "We'll all be witnesses."

"What will it prove?" asked Mr. Gavin, his brow cocked. "Only that one is fake and one is real. I said the same. He had a copy made." Mr. Gavin jabbed a finger at Bill Mason.

Bill shook his head. "I wouldn't know how to do it or where. I also didn't have the opportunity."

"I believe you," said Chuck.

Libby did too, but she didn't speak, only smiled at Bill.

Mr. Page moved restlessly. "Let's get on with it!"

Libby stepped closer to Chuck as Cam took the unicorn from Chuck and laid it on the counter. Cam opened the case and pulled out the other unicorn.

"Side-by-side they do look just alike," Cam said in disbelief.

Carefully Cam dripped nitric acid on the unicorns and watched the bubbles.

Libby wrinkled her nose at the terrible smell of the acid.

"This one is gold and copper," said Cam, pointing to the unicorn Libby had had. "I'll cut into the other to see if it's only gold plated like I think it is."

Libby watched as Cam did the test. She felt Mr. Gavin's tension. She glanced at Bill, and he was watching the test as intently as the others. Just outside the door the guard was holding the next class back. They were laughing and talking.

"Just as I thought," said Cam as he rubbed the acid off the unicorn. "It is gold plated. The value of this unicorn is less than fifty dollars."

"I'll call the sheriff and have Mason arrested," said Mr. Gavin crisply.

"I'm innocent," said Bill, looking at Chuck for support.

"I think we should look at the motive to see who's guilty," said Chuck. "The unicorn alone is nothing compared to the value of the entire collection."

Libby puffed up with pride as Chuck talked about the Josef Mueller collection and who'd want it.

"Why was the unicorn put on display here when you knew the danger was so great?" asked Chuck.

Mr. Gavin shrugged. "I felt it was important for boys and girls to see it."

"I know this is the only school it's to be shown at," said Cam. "That seems strange to me."

"Probably no other school had an ex-con as a janitor's helper," said Bill grimly. "A perfect suspect."

"I believe you're right," said Chuck. "We'll see who approved the showing of the unicorn here, and we'll have the criminal."

"He did," said Cam, nodding at Mr. Gavin.

Mr. Gavin flushed. "That doesn't prove a thing!"

"We'll let the police decide," said Mr. Page.

Suddenly Mr. Gavin grabbed the valuable unicorn and ran toward the exit. As he started past Libby she stuck her foot out and tripped him. He landed flat on his face, and the unicorn fell from his hand. Libby scooped it up and handed it back to Cam.

Chuck smiled at Libby, and she felt ten feet tall. The others praised her quick action, making her flush with embarrassment.

Mr. Gavin slowly pushed himself up, suddenly looking old and tired. "I need the unicorn," he whispered. "I promised Dad I'd get it for him. Dad's an art collector. He spent most of his life getting the other charms—the Pegasus and the mermaid. All he needed was the unicorn and the nymph. When I got the job at the museum, he begged me to switch the real unicorn for a forged one. He seemed desperate, so I told him I'd do it."

"You did plan the switch at this school because of me, didn't you?" asked Bill angrily.

Mr. Gavin nodded. "It got too complicated, especially when the real one disappeared."

Libby hung her head. Could she tell them her terrible secret? Finally she said, "I thought it was lucky, so I wanted to keep it. I'm sorry."

Mr. Page stepped forward and took Mr. Gavin by the arm. "I think it's time to call the police," he said, "and the museum authorities. As you've so often insisted, Mr. Gavin, the real thief needs to be punished."

Mr. Gavin looked down, ashamed. Libby almost felt sorry for him as Mr. Page and Cam led him away.

Chuck tightened his arm around Libby, and she felt better.

Later Libby walked to the parking lot with Chuck and Bill. When they reached Chuck's pickup truck, she turned to Bill. "I saw Mr. Gavin giving you some money a while ago. I thought you might be helping him steal the unicorn."

Bill laughed. "Not a chance! He was paying me for sweet rolls I'd picked up for his crew."

"It's very important never to jump to conclusions," said Chuck.

Libby nodded. Suddenly she remembered her science test. She didn't dare miss it. "Dad, I have to get to class. See you after school." She hugged him, and he kissed her cheek.

"I love you, Elizabeth," whispered Chuck.

"I love you, Dad." Libby waved to Bill then ran toward the door. Even without the unicorn she knew she'd do well on her science test. Not because of luck—but because she'd studied and because God was always with her to help her. She smiled. "I love you, heavenly Father!"

ABOUT THE AUTHOR

Hilda Stahl was born and raised in the Nebraska Sandhills. When she was a young teen she realized she needed a personal relationship with God, so she accepted Christ into her life. She attended a Bible college where she met her husband, Norman. They and their seven children now live in Michigan.

When Hilda was a young mother with three children, she saw an ad in a magazine for a correspondence course in writing. She took the test, passed it, and soon fell in love with being a writer. She would write whenever she had free time, and she eventually began to sell what she wrote.

Hilda now has books with Tyndale House Publishers (the Elizabeth Gail series, The Tina series, The Teddy Jo series, and the Tyler Twins series), Accent Books (the Wren House mystery series), Bethel Publishing (the Amber Ainslie detective series, and *Gently Touch Sheela Jenkins,* a book for adults on child abuse), and Crossway Books (the Super JAM series for boys and *Sadie Rose and the Daring Escape,* for which she won the 1989 Angel Award). Hilda also has had hundreds of short stories published and has written a radio script for the Children's Bible Hour.

Some of Hilda's books have been translated into foreign languages, including Dutch, Chinese, and Hebrew. And when her first Elizabeth Gail book, *The Mystery at the Johnson Farm,* was made into a movie in 1989, it was a real dream come true for Hilda. She wants her books and their message of God's love and power to reach and help people all over the world. Hilda's writing centers on the truth that no matter what we may experience or face in life, Christ is always the answer.

Hilda speaks on writing at schools and organizations, and she is an instructor for the Institute of Children's Literature. She continues to write, teach, and speak—but mostly to write, because that is what she feels God has called her to do.

If you've enjoyed the **Elizabeth Gail** *series,*
double your fun with these delightful heroines!

Anika Scott

#1 The Impossible Lisa Barnes

#2 Tianna the Terrible

Cassie Perkins

#1 No More Broken Promises

#2 A Forever Friend

#3 A Basket of Roses

#4 A Dream to Cherish

#5 The Much-Adored Sandy Shore

#6 Love Burning Bright

You can find Tyndale books at fine bookstores everywhere.
If you are unable to find these titles at your local bookstore,
you may write for order information to:

Tyndale House Publishers
Tyndale Family Products Dept.
Box 448
Wheaton, IL 60189